The Yellow Bird Sings

The Yellow Bird Sings

Jennifer Rosner

FLATIRON
BOOKS
NEW YORK

Hide/seek portion of homily on page 145 adapted from "Epiphany O Godhead Hid" by Geoffrey Foot, January 1, 2018.

This is a work of fiction. All of the characters, organizations, and events portrayed in this novel are either products of the author's imagination or are used fictitiously. The town names Gracja and Celestyn are fictional names. Any resemblance to real town names is purely coincidental.

THE YELLOW BIRD SINGS. Copyright © 2020 by Jennifer Rosner. All rights reserved. Printed in the United States of America. For information, address Flatiron Books, 120 Broadway, New York, N.Y. 10271.

www.flatironbooks.com

The Library of Congress Cataloging-in-Publication Data is available upon request.

ISBN 978-1-250-83330-3

Our books may be purchased in bulk for promotional, educational, or business use. Please contact your local bookseller or the Macmillan Corporate and Premium Sales Department at 1-800-221-7945, ext. 5442, or by e-mail at MacmillanSpecialMarkets@macmillan.com.

First U.S Edition: 2020
First Flatiron Trade Paperback Edition: 2021
First Flatiron Mass Market Edition: February 2022

10 9 8 7 6 5 4 3 2 1

For my parents

Part 1

The girl is forbidden from making a sound, so the yellow bird sings. He sings whatever the girl composes in her head: high-pitched trills of piccolo; low-throated growls of contrabassoon. The bird chirps all the musical parts save percussion, because the barn rabbits obligingly thump their back feet like bass drums, like snares. The lines for violin and cello are the most elaborately composed. Rich and liquid smooth, except when fear turns the notes gruff and choppy.

Music helps the flowers bloom. When the daisies grow abundant, the bird weaves a garland for the girl to wear on her head like a princess—though no one can see. She must hide from everyone in the village: soldiers, the farmhouse boys, the neighbors too. The lady with squinty eyes and blocky shoes just dragged a boy down the street and returned, smug and straight-backed, cradling a sack of sugar like a baby.

When giants tromp past, the bird holes up in a knot in the rafter, silent and still. Tending the garden must wait. The girl, music trapped inside, buries herself under hay. She imagines her mother whispering their nightly story or whisper-singing her favorite lullaby. She holds tight to her blanket and tries to fall asleep, sniffing in vain for the faded scent of home.

Chapter 1

Poland
Summer 1941

A brooding heat permeates the tight space of the barn loft, no larger than three strides by four. The boards are rough-hewn and splintery and the rafters run at sharp slants, making the pitch too low for Róża to stand anywhere but in the center. Silken webs wad the corners and thin shards of sunlight bleed through cracks. Otherwise it is dark.

Kneeling, Róża pats down a dense pad of hay for Shira to lie on. She positions her by the wall across from the ladder, then covers her with more hay. Róża makes a spot for herself in front of her daughter, angled so she can keep her eyes on the door. Her heart still hammers in her chest.

Not an hour ago Henryk's wife, Krystyna, barreled in to corner a chicken and discovered them crouching behind a hay cart. Róża swallowed a startled gasp and tightened her hold on Shira. Krystyna's eyes darted to the wall hung with tools—trowels and spades, shovels, a pitchfork—then she slowly backed out. A few moments later Henryk stepped in. His expression was deeply troubled, but his hands held two potatoes each.

"We have boys of our own. We'll all be killed."

The dirt-packed floor shuddered beneath Róża's feet. There were *prizes* for denunciations: a bag of sugar per Jew. Her mind raced with what currency she could offer: yeast and salt from the bakery. Coins. Three of her grandmother's rubies sewn into the hem of a coat. If necessary, her wedding ring.

Had she misjudged them? Henryk frequented their bakery before the war. He had been friendly, maybe even a little flirtatious, when Róża worked at the counter. Sometimes he brought his son Piotr and each would eat a jam-filled cookie in one bite, smiling and batting away the powdered sugar that clung to their lips. They were grateful to her family; her uncle Jakob, a medical doctor, tended to Piotr when he came down with rubella. Róża believed they'd help, at least at the start.

"I beg you, just for a night or two."

"No more."

Henryk cleared equipment from the loft and forked up hay. Róża followed closely as Shira scampered up the ladder.

Now they lie here, still and silent. Róża asks herself, *Where will we go next?* Not back to Gracja. Not after what happened to Natan, shot dead after a week's hard labor, and her parents, herded out of their apartment onto cattle trucks. And not to the woods, where her cousin Leyb has gone, with no guarantee of food or shelter. Come winter, with the forest's frigid temperatures, Shira could not survive it.

So *where*? Róża scours her mind but finds no answer. Tonight's contingency is Henryk's root cellar, to the side of the farmhouse, if vacating the barn becomes necessary.

The loft boards are hard on Róża's back and buttocks, and a splinter of hay stabs at her neck, yet she holds still until Shira drifts to sleep; then she shifts position, ever so slightly, in a slow, soundless motion.

In the afternoon, Henryk places a water bucket and two clean rags inside the barn door. Róża and Shira pad silently down the ladder. After they drink their fill, Róża submerges her arms in the water, the coolness loosening her whole being.

She wipes Shira clean first, taking the dirt and grime from her cheeks and neck with slow, gentle turns of the cloth. Patiently, indulgently, she swabs Shira's hands—cupped tight as if cradling something, a habit started after her father didn't return—moving the cloth quickly between each of Shira's fingers, then sponging her wrists and upper arms. She sends Shira flitting up to the loft and begins on herself, unbuttoning her shirt to reach her chest, her back, and the space under her arms. The water trickles down her sides; Róża catches it with the cloth and carries it upward along her body, taking care to rub away her odor. She sponges until she senses a slight shift outside the barn. *Henryk?* He lingered after delivering the bucket, she thinks, and is now watching her through a crack in the lower barn wall. Her breath grows shallow. She looks down at her exposed breasts, her taut stomach, her jutting hips. Her first instinct is to turn away, but she holds herself still. They will be fed here tonight. Sheltered. She douses the cloth again and continues on, the feel of Henryk's eyes watching her, seeing her.

Later in the day, Róża peers through a gap in the loft boards and glimpses Krystyna inside the farmhouse, agitated, arguing with Henryk. She is shaking her head, hard, causing the baby, Łukasz, to slip sideways down her hip. Róża sinks low to the loft floor.

Henryk enters the barn and begins forking hay out in large piles, blocking the sight line from the neighboring fields and the road.

The farmhouse, white with carved shutters painted a cheery blue, is smaller than the barn and does not fully occlude the view from the road, especially where it curves. The tavern must be somewhere close by because already Róża can hear carousing.

At nightfall Róża shows Shira how to wrap her finger in the clean corner of a rag to make a toothbrush and how to relieve herself in a bucket filled with straw that Henryk will afterward mix with the animals' hay and waste.

Henryk brings a different bucket with food in it. Boiled cabbage and turnips. "Krystyna sent this for you. Just for tonight. She's very frightened."

Róża nods, grateful.

Back beneath hay, Róża presses the heels of her hands to her eyes. Spots of yellow and black bloom there, spreading like spilled dye. They chase away images of Natan and her parents.

Eventually, she opens her eyes to find Shira watching, enchanted, as two rabbits hop sideways on a hay bale and scurry about. If Shira misses her bedtime rituals from home—a drawn bath, warm milk with nutmeg and honey, snuggles from her grandparents—she doesn't show it. On her leg, her fingers tap out the rhythm to some elaborate melody only she hears in her head.

Krystyna enters an hour later, stern and stiff postured, her lips pulled into a straight line. But she's brought more water and a bit of bread. Róża can neither thank Krystyna nor admonish Shira before her girl flits down the loft ladder and, with a dramatic bow, offers Krystyna a small rectangle of woven hay she's made. Krystyna's face softens. Her eyes grow kind. Shira scrambles back to the loft and into Róża's arms.

Chapter 2

Shira practices being invisible. She hunches her shoulders, sucks in her stomach, slinks like a cat. Her mother practices, too, burying herself deep in the hay and beckoning Shira, with a wave of her hand, to settle into her lap and be still. Or with a finger to her lips, she instructs her to stay silent.

The floorboards are rough and the hay is sharp and scratchy. Shira does not understand why they can't go home—why they ever *left* home—where together her mother and father tucked her into bed as if in a soft, downy nest and where music and the scent of her grandmother's baking wafted through the air.

There, Shira could patter down the hall and join the company, watching as they unclasped the cases of their instruments. Nestled in her grandfather's lap, breathing in his workshop smells of sawdust and lacquer, she bounced and tapped to the ripple of notes from her mama's cello, her *tata*'s violin.

At first, in the tuning and warm-up, everything sounded off-kilter and sad. But then they struck up their songs and the music carried them all, until Shira no longer felt herself

settled against her grandfather but in an altogether different place of pure, shared beauty. Vibrant, soulful melodies.
Fiery, stomping rhythms. It didn't matter how loud things
got—there wasn't a neighbor in the building who didn't rel-
ish their playing. Shira could even hum if she wanted to. But
here, her mother is insistent: they need to be silent, to hide.
So she coils herself tight like a spring and holds herself in.

Shira strives to mute the sound of every movement—
her footfalls, her breath. The anticipated stream of her pee,
she has learned to mete out in a near-silent trickle. And
she knows to cover over and so erase any sign of her exis-
tence—a series of vanishing moments—before she retreats
beneath piles of hay.

Yet even as Shira wills herself to silence, her body de-
fies her with a sudden sneeze, an involuntary swallow, the
loud crack of her hip from being still too long. A calf muscle
cramps. An itch needs a scratch. Her bowels press. The most
carefully planned movement causes the hay to rustle or a
floorboard to whine. Shira looks over at her mother apologetically. Worried, her mother stares back.

Shira rehearses the plan to move, if need be, from the barn
to the root cellar—a *ziemianka* with the stork's nest above
it, at the side of the farmhouse—where she is to wait for her
mother on the floor behind the barrels, unmoving (no matter
the cold or damp) for however long it takes: neck straight,
not crooked, or else she'll get sore. She also rehearses what
her mother told her over and over about her sounds, how they
can be no louder than a whisper except when she says that
it is safe, very late at night, to speak pianissimo rather than
piano pianissimo. If her mother wakes her suddenly, she is
not to raise her voice. She must control her breathing: no
heaving sighs. Absolutely no sneezes.

Whenever Shira so much as shifts her weight, the floor-board creaks and the air grows thick and humid, hard to breathe. But then her yellow bird skitters out of her hands and scuttles through a hole in the loft boards. He darts about, looking for danger, and returns with his bright feathers ruffled by the wind. Shira searches his bead-black eyes and finds reassurance: *Her sounds went unheard.*

She settles back into the hay and tries again to be still until notes, snippets of song, and soon whole passages take shape and pulse through her, quiet at first, then building in intensity and growing louder. A story told with strings and woodwinds: a glacial night, a flickering fire, sounds like black water beneath bright ice, basses and timpani and a violin's yearnings, and, finally, a crescendo, the frozen earth cracking—

Her mother waves an arm, her forehead furrowed. Shira realizes she is tapping again.

Chapter 3

Time blurs and swells in the barn. The day's hiding is indistinguishable from the night's, and the tick of each silent minute feels like an eternity in the shadowy darkness. Yet Róża continues with the sleep-time routine she started for Shira when they first ran from Gracja, when they kept to the outskirts of villages, crossing fields and meadows on their way to Henryk's barn.

First they peer at the photographs in the card fold: Natan at university in an image grainy and dark; Róża's parents, soft eyed despite their stiff, formal postures; and Shira in her ankle-length dress. Róża wishes she could have grabbed other photographs, better ones of Natan and of their extended family. But these were in reach.

In whispers, Shira asks Róża to tell her about each one.

"This is your papa the day he earned his pharmacology degree; this is your *bobe* and *zayde* at Aunt Syl and Uncle Jakob's wedding; this is you at cousin Gavriel's bar mitzvah."

Then Róża tells the story of a little girl who, with the help of her bright yellow bird, tends an enchanted garden. The little girl is five years old, the same age as Shira. The garden must be kept silent—only birdsong is safe—yet there is a princess who can't stop sneezing and giants who must never hear them. There are adventures and threats averted by the little girl's quick thinking; and each time, the story ends with the girl and her mother curled together in a soft heap of daisy petals for a good night's sleep.

Afterward, Róża whisper-sings a lullaby about chicks waiting for their mother to return home with glasses of tea to drink. She leaves out the *Cucuricoo* that starts off the lullaby and prays Shira won't utter it aloud. Then she folds her large fingers over Shira's small ones—a hugging of hands, a good-night squeeze—and settles Shira to sleep with her blanket.

Only tonight, addled from hunger, inactivity, and the fading purple light, Róża nods off in the middle of telling the story. She jolts awake, clarity renewed, when she hears the sound of someone entering the barn. Henryk. He carries the night air and the scent of alcohol up the ladder, into the loft.

Róża guesses it is after midnight. The farmhouse is unlit: Krystyna and the boys must be sleeping. Shira sits cross-legged in the very center of the loft, wide-awake, pretending to play with her bird, trying to decipher Henryk's whisperings of war news he just heard in the tavern.

Henryk's eyes dart in Shira's direction. "When does she sleep?"

Róża prods Shira to a place by the wall farthest from the ladder. "I need you to lie here. Yes, with your face toward the wall, no turning—here's your blanket—and I promise I will finish our story first thing in the morning." Róża feels Shira bristle at the false brightness in her voice.

"But Mama—"

"No questions now. *Shh.*"

Róża stays silent and unmoving as Henryk fumbles her pants down and pushes his way inside her. Dry and tight, she feels as if she is ripping. His weight is heavy upon her. His thrusts grow faster, deeper, the pounding harder and harder. Hay cuts into her back as he presses her into the floorboards, his salt and sweat and breath in her nose.

His sounds, the sound of them—the battering of a porch door in a rainstorm—could give everything away. Yet Róża can do nothing but wait for it to be over. Henryk feels up her shirt and finds her nipple; he twists, squeezing it hard. Róża locks her eyes on a crack in the loft wall, a shard of moonlight. Henryk continues to push. A final grunt and the hot wet fill of him inside, before he collapses on top of her, one hand still in her hair.

When Róża dares to look Shira's way, she recognizes at once, from the uneven movement of her girl's breath, that she is still awake.

Early the next morning, their second day in the barn, Róża is up and frantic about vacating—where will they go?—when Henryk steps in. She straightens, crosses her arms around her middle.

"You can stay a bit longer," Henryk says.

Róża drops like a puddle into the hay. "Thank you."

Later, she watches as a neighbor saunters over with a plate of sugar cookies and interrupts Henryk chiding his older boys, Piotr and Jurek. He'd told them to stay away from the well pump, but they'd fiddled with it and it broke. Now he's *warning* them—keep out of the barn.

"Did you get a horse?" the neighbor asks, cookies aloft, eyes squinting.

"Huh?"

"A horse in your barn?" Tall piles of hay still block the sight line from the neighboring fields to the front face of the barn.

"Oh that. No, I've just been moving equipment around, that's all."

When another neighbor approaches, Krystyna—her eyes only once flitting upward toward the loft—carries little Łukasz to the group to be exclaimed over. What instinct to protect Róża and Shira has come to bear in her? Róża wonders. And what instinct to betray might arise as instantly?

Róża pulls away from the wall crack before she witnesses any of them eating the cookies.

The day unfolds: Krystyna brings a jar of water and two pieces of bread; later, Henryk removes their waste pail. Despite these kindnesses, Róża is certain that, at any moment, one or the other will demand they leave—and she racks her brain, trying to think of where she and Shira might go next. There is a house she knows, next village over, where she once delivered a *sękacz* for a merchant's wedding. The cake—forty eggs' worth—was tall like a tree and difficult to carry; and the house stood out because it, too, was very tall. She tries to remember: How near was the house to its neighbors? And did she ever hear news that the merchant's wife had children? If so, they may have less luck there. . . .

At nightfall, Krystyna brings soup. Neither she nor Henryk mention them leaving. After they eat, Róża beds Shira down for the night, telling a new installment of the story. The little girl discovers a family of moles, gently poking one another with their noses and scuffling about in a hole near the garden! The girl fears the moles will tunnel through a bed of enchanted flowers, so she smartly composes a "moving song" for her bird to sing to them. Upon hearing the jaunty tune, the moles don their hats, reach for their rucksacks, and scurry off, heads bobbing to the music—and the garden is safe. Shira asks: "What do the moles carry in their rucksacks?" Róża answers: "Their eyeglasses!" Shira's own eyes grow wide with delighted wonder. Then Róża whisper-sings the lullaby, folds her hands over Shira's hands, and tucks her in with her blanket—all before Henryk scales the ladder.

They are not kicked out of the barn the day after or the day after that. Róża carves shallow nicks in the barn rafter with a rock to keep track of each day. She likes the weight of the rock in her hand, the give of the soft wood beneath. In the accumulation of marks she feels the triumph of survival, tempered always by fear.

Chapter 4

As Róża marks the rafter, another day's end, Shira whispers her persistent questions: "Why must we hide? Why must we stay silent?" Róża fixes Shira with her eyes, wishing she had answers that would still her.

"Some giants don't like flowers, and because they believe the music in our voices helps the flowers grow, we must never let the giants hear our songs."

"Is it all right for a bird to sing?"

"Yes, so long as *we* stay silent."

Róża turns back to the rafter, thinking of Henryk's visit the previous night. He moved inside her slowly, almost gently. She couldn't help noting his differences from Natan: the very heft of him, how his chest has less hair, how his smell holds the earth's tang in it. Even as she kept herself entirely still—looking on as if from a different body, a different place—her eyes wandered from the wall to his face, his sloping gray eyes—

The sharp point of the rock, clenched in Róża's fist, bites at her flesh. She swallows a yelp and sets the rock down in the corner. She calculates back, trying to figure out which nick Shabbas fell on, unobserved.

Maybe the merchant's wife lives by herself in the tall house? Unlike Henryk, who is exempt because of an eye nerve problem that keeps him from clearing his vision quickly in smoke, the husband has likely been conscripted.

Counting the nicks, Róża sees it is their eleventh day in the barn.

Chapter 5

Shira and her mother don't speak during the day, the nineteenth day, when sunlight streams through cracks in the wallboards, dappling patches of their skin a luminous white. Even Henryk's treat of an extra baked potato can elicit no words of thanks. Only her mother's flat smile as she watches Shira soundlessly devouring it.

In the silence, other sounds are pronounced. Inside the barn, the rustle, thump, and nibbling of rabbits. Outside, the morning calls of the wrens and the rose finch. The whispering leaves. The slap and crunch of Henryk's boots. And late, late at night, when Shira is to stay especially still, the high creak and shift of the barn door. The scrape of the ladder against the floorboards. The distinctive groan of each rung, then the hushed tones of Henryk, up in the loft with her mother.

Henryk carries outdoor smells with him to the loft. Sometimes there are leafy bits from his boots. He mumbles words that Shira cannot hear. Her mother gives Shira the card fold of photographs to hold, enclosed in her blanket, as she nods and mumbles back to him. When Henryk is there, Shira must lie apart from her mother, turned away and confused by the commotion.

Some evenings, Shira hears soldiers walking along the road. If they have been drinking, they sing about kissing pretty girls, songs that Shira secretly enjoys. Otherwise, sharp footfalls and talk.

When it is too dangerous even for whispers, Shira and her mother gesture. A simple finger near the ear means *I hear someone*, but more particular signs denote Henryk (the tug of a beard), his wife, Krystyna (the tying of apron strings), and the three Wiśniewski boys (oldest to youngest, a hand upon a child's head at high, middle, and low heights). A neighbor (palms facing, held near). Soldiers (fists clenched at the chest, as if around a gun). A stranger, they don't know who (eyebrows raised). Taps on different body parts show hunger, thirst, pain, a full bladder. A hand on a clump of hair, *Do you want a braid?* It passes a bit of time. A brush of the fingers over closing eyelids, *Try to rest now.* Shira watches her mother's lips shape prayers in Hebrew before falling off to sleep. This, more than anything, calms Shira, for in her mind she hears her mother's silent chants as music.

They wear their shoes always, in case they need to run. Shira's shoes crush her pinkie toes, but she doesn't tell. She doesn't tell about the hay splinters in her fingers either, or about the way she feels hungry all the time. Her mother gives her the larger portion of everything they get to eat. If Shira ever offers her mother more, she never takes it; she sucks on hay instead. The soft, fleshy parts of her are gone. Shira can see her mother's collarbones jutting out.

Shira wears the dress Krystyna snuck in for her, outgrown by her niece, with its pretty checkered pattern and gray trim. It isn't soft like the dresses in her closet at home, sewn by her grandmother, fitting just right, and almost as wonderful as the ones in the shop windows in Gracja. Her mother wears a pair of pants cinched at the waist and a wide-collared shirt—clothes for traveling, she says. Together, they lie silent in the hay, inhaling its layered scents—sweet, sharp, dank, and rotting—and listen to the sounds of the night. A screech and a whistle. A dog's bark.

Shira met a dog as she and her mother crossed the pastures near Henryk's barn. Her mother sought to shoo the dog away, fearful that he would bark. But Shira put out her hand. The dog tilted his head and sniffed, his nose twitching, his eyes flickering with golds and yellows, his felted ears dropping back. He seemed to understand, even to share with Shira this project of invisibility. Dodging to the side, he trotted off as if weightless, not even the slightest tap-tap as he padded along the road. Shira imagined him carrying a wordless message to her father.

Shira watches through a crack in the boards as Henryk plays with Łukasz outside, zooming him through the air. Łukasz squeals and reaches out a chubby hand to grasp at Henryk's puckered lips, to rub his whiskers against the grain.

There had been evenings, after her mother unstraddled her legs from around her cello and set to tidying the kitchen, that Shira's father lifted her on his lap and showed her how to form whole scales' worth of notes by pressing different places on the violin strings. His voice, low and close, reminded Shira of water: creeks and rivers, the whisper of tides. Eagerly, she stretched her fingers across the strings, as far as they would reach, and he sounded out her notes with long, smooth bow strokes. Sometimes he let her try to hold the violin all by herself, clasping the smooth wooden neck between her thumb and forefinger, placing her chin on the big oblong rest. When she set her fingers to quivering upon the strings as she'd seen her parents do, to make a vibrato, her father laughed, the sound like a tumbling spring, his breath the scent of coffee, moist upon her cheek.

Does Shira truly remember her father, gray speckled and musky, his embrace warm and soft but not like her mama's, or is she making him up, mixing him up with her visions and dreams? A star-backed violin at his bearded chin, notes undulating like a tuning fork come to pierce her mother's heart. The dancing stopped short, the violin boxed and buried after he didn't return. Upon waking, the thought that if she could just lie with an ear to the ground, she might hear her father's notes floating up through the rooted earth.

To ask about him would cause her mother to fold in upon herself like a paper swan. So Shira bites her lips and closes her eyes against the scene outside.

Shira and her mother devise silent games. Guess how many swallows are nesting in the barn. Count the knotholes in the wallboards. When it is time to sleep, Shira snuggles close, hands cupped, as her mother begins the story.

Tonight a white-spotted deer has entered the garden, hoping to feast on enchanted flowers. The little girl and her bird fear (rightly) that a giant will want to eat the deer for dinner, so they devise a plan: the girl conducts and the bird chirps a pastorale of bleating fawn calls. The deer lifts her head, alerted—she's sure her baby is calling—and scampers off just as the giant's thundering steps can be heard in the distance.

Shira begs her mother to continue—she loves imagining the girl and her bird in the garden with white daisies, with deer and symphonies, dark sounds to warn of danger—but her mother is firm.

"Tomorrow, Shirke. We'll have to wait and see what excitement comes tomorrow."

Her mother whispers her lullaby, and Shira stretches out her hands, watching as her mother's fingers fold over hers like a promise. Then she settles with her hay-coated shred of blanket and Shira drifts off to sleep, listening as always for the sound of footsteps.

Chapter 6

While Shira sleeps, Róża lies motionless beneath mounds of hay, straining to hear the world outside the barn. The distant clop of horses. Indistinct voices from the tavern down the road.

People pass by day and night; yet no matter how Róża tries, she cannot keep Shira entirely silent and still. It is hardest in the morning when Shira first wakes. Róża must constantly signal. A finger to the mouth: *Be quiet.* A hand to the leg: *Don't move.* Shira chews on her lips in response, yet her every breath, her every swallow, seems to ring out.

The hours stretch before them, endless, and each minute demands vigilance as Shira's imagination flutters and darts and her body pulses, irrepressibly, with song.

Along their journey here, on the far outskirts of villages, Róża could permit Shira's humming and tapping. Her tunes—startlingly complex and layered, notes merging and colliding—reminded Róża of the symphonies her father had listened to.

"What music is that?" Róża had asked Shira.

"Hmm?"

"What you're humming—"

"Oh. Just what I hear in my head."

How Róża wishes Shira could continue, recognizing her talent and knowing what solace it brings her—but not now. "It's lovely, but you must keep it *inside* you."

Róża wishes Shira would keep her constant, whispered questions—"Mama, why are we here? Where is *Tata*? Can we go home soon?"—inside her too.

Henryk and Krystyna would not denounce them—their fates were by now entwined—but a neighbor might hear. With a tip-off, German soldiers would come searching.

The one time Henryk pronounced a leave date, conferencing with Krystyna in low tones by the chicken coop, out of earshot from neighbors and the children, it met with Krystyna's unexpected petition, "Where will they go, Henryk? The girl can't be much older than Maryla's little Łucja." At that time—the thirty-second day in the barn by the count of nicks in the rafter, and all her barter goods given, gone— Róża could feel only the luck of Krystyna's plea. Yet she has cause to doubt Krystyna now, as she steps up the loft ladder and reaches a hand toward Shira.

Róża scans the loft, fearful that Shira's sleep pad, shoved all the way to the side, will give away what Henryk does here at night. But Krystyna doesn't seem to notice.

"Why don't I take her out for a bit? She needs fresh air."

Róża grips Shira, tight. *What? No!* "Thank you, but it's far too dangerous."

"Just a little walk. A few steps to see the chickens. The sun is hardly up yet."

Róża flushes hot despite the crisp air. The way the farm is set, on a long, narrow swath of land, the chicken coop sits close by the barn, fields running behind. Even with the hay still piled up outside, someone might see to the coop from the curved point in the road. She doesn't want to anger Krystyna, but she can't possibly let Shira go. "I don't think it's a good idea."

"Mama, I want to see the chickens!"

"Shh!"

Róża searches Krystyna's face.

"Henryk has taken the boys to his parents'. As for our neighbors, Ludwika is at her sister's and Borys is sleeping off his night at the tavern."

"What if soldiers pass by? Or other neighbors . . ." The one who baked sugar cookies.

Krystyna glances in the direction of the road. "The hay blocks the view." A pause. "I just can't imagine if one of my boys had to lie still and silent for so long."

A small barn swallow flutters in the eaves. Róża feels Shira wriggling from her grasp.

Sweat breaks and gathers beneath Róża's arms. She has seen the way Shira envies Jurek and Piotr tromping in and out of the coops, their hair wet. What if Krystyna is right, that Shira needs to move about more? She grows unsure and Shira sidles toward Krystyna. Together they move down the ladder and out the barn door, toward the coop.

Róża's heart batters in the cage of her chest as she shifts between cracks in the wall, glimpsing her child in fragments: Shira's cocked head, her left leg, a dangling hand. When they step into the coop, disappearing entirely from view, Róża starts to count, one, two, three, four, five, six . . .

Distraught, she picks up Shira's blanket, runs her finger over the seam. She could sew Shira's name there, tiny stitches, in case they were ever parted. She could ask Krystyna to borrow needle and thread—

She puts the blanket down. *Where* are *they?* She peers through the largest crack, desperate for the sight of her child.

They reappear and in a few steps they are back in the barn. The whole outing, less than five minutes. Despite her relief, Róża flares with anger. She'd barely breathed while Shira was gone.

"There will be chicks in the spring!" Shira's voice trills.

"Quiet!"

"Yes, Mama," she whispers.

Krystyna stands just inside the door as Shira scuttles up the ladder. Róża rakes her into her arms and tries to regularize her breathing.

A few days later Krystyna comes back, again before sunrise. Róża strains against the dull light to watch as Krystyna leads Shira by the hand to see the chickens, a bit farther to pet the cow. Even as she keeps vigil, her eyes trained on Shira's every movement, Róża feels grateful for these few moments alone.

Krystyna sets out a small basket of food behind the hay pile that blocks the barn. Róża squints, straining to see: Hard-boiled eggs? Slices of bread? She wants Shira back—but she is eating.

Róża's stomach rumbles; saliva pools in her mouth. When she thinks Krystyna sees her watching, she shifts and peers through a different, tinier crack.

Krystyna abruptly packs up the food.

Is someone passing by on the road?

Róża listens for the clomp of boots as Krystyna leads Shira back to the barn, up the loft ladder, into Róża's arms. Róża inhales the scent of bread on Shira's lips.

* * *

Beneath the hay, Róża lies beside Shira, her hand gently running over the child's full belly.

"I wanted to bring food for you, Mama, but Pani Wiśniewska took it away."

"It's all right, Shirke. I'm glad you had good things to eat."

"She said that Pan Wiśniewski would bring you potatoes later."

Róża is silent.

"I wanted to bring an egg for you! I promise to, next time."

"No talking now." Róża swallows hard, on nothing.

Later, Róża takes Shira into her lap and parts her thick hair into three even clumps. With the separated hair clasped between her fingers, she begins to braid, weaving the strands over and under, each cross marked with a gentle tug, until just wisps remain. With Shira's hair pulled back, her resemblance to her grandmother, olive toned and heart shaped, is acute. Except for her eyes, the shape and color of almonds, like Natan's.

"I've made your hair especially fancy today. Just as it will be when I take you to see the Philharmonic."

Shira turns to look at her, disbelieving.

"That's right. When we can go home, we'll splurge for seats and you'll hear the symphony."

Shira pats the braid that cascades down the nape of her neck.

Róża thinks back to concerts she attended as a girl with her parents. Dressed in their best, they still looked shabby compared with most of the other concertgoers, but it didn't matter because her father had *made* several of the violins that were played there. Afterward, Róża was permitted to join her parents, late, at the kitchen table for tea and linzer torte.

Róża ties off Shira's braid with a fresh strand of hay as the barn tints with the pale purple light of dusk. She drapes her arms around her girl and drifts into fitful, hungry sleep.

Chapter 7

Shira knows her mama prefers her to stay holed up, but the excitement of walking outside—feeling the fresh air on her face and in her hair, darting among the chickens as they strut and peck, and then getting hard-boiled eggs to eat—builds, so that every time she sees Krystyna approaching the barn, Shira sits up, hopeful. She yearns so badly to go, just the few steps between the barn and the coop, with Krystyna's firm hand on her back all the while.

Her *tata* would understand. Last birthday, he set up a whole scavenger hunt for her, up and down the riverbank. If he were here, she knows: he would want to go too.

As her mother sleeps, Shira pats the top of her bird's fluffy yellow head and feeds him tiny droplets of nectar from her littlest finger, wondering what story adventures await them tonight. His heart beats heavy and quick. With each new sound outside—the stomp of boots, the rise of voices—he burrows deeper into the nest of Shira's hands.

"Now, now," she whispers.

They both know there are other birds outside the barn, huddled in tree holes, hidden by branches, hunched beneath sticks and pine needles. Is *his tata* out there somewhere, searching for him? Even the wild birds don't dare make a peep. They'll sound their calls at dawn when the men are in their houses, in their beds, too slow and groggy to step into their boots.

She'll be his company for now, and he'll be hers. She needs him, especially as dreams drive her mother into a restless state, shifting upon the floorboards and calling out. Shira asks herself: *Should I shake Mama awake? Or let her sleep on?* Her bird hops and pecks, urging Shira to put a hand upon her mother's cheek, halt the dreams that haunt her.

Shira's bird stays with her when Krystyna takes her out of the barn, and when the warning footsteps of soldiers prompt Shira and her mother to bury themselves entirely beneath the hay. And he stays with her when Henryk pounds up the ladder. When she is meant to be her most quiet. Meant to be sleeping.

When Shira is happy, as she was when her mother showed her how to make stitches with the needle and thread Krystyna brought them, he perches in the barn rafters or on a mound of hay nearby. But when she is upset, as she was when she poked her finger and blood dripped onto the hem of her dress, he flies straight into her cupped hands.

He could chirp if he wanted to. His call is wondrous—eighteen warbling notes long. But he stays silent. Such a sound as that might draw attention, and just now, they have to hide.

Chapter 8

Papa told us not to go in. Piotr—"

"You don't have to come."

This is all the warning Róża has that the older boys are at the barn door. Quickly, she buries Shira and herself beneath hay and silently prays, *Please, let Shira be still; let her not shift or sigh or tap or sneeze . . .*

The door scrapes open. With the boys' entry, a trapeze of sunlight. "We're going to get in trouble!" Jurek says.

"I don't know why Papa forbade us. There's nothing even in here."

"We should invite the girls."

"I thought you were worried about getting in trouble!"

"Well, it could be worth it for that. It smells bad, though."

"Where is that coming from?"

"Maybe up there—should we check it out?"

Róża's heart pounds so violently, she's sure the boys can hear it. If they climb into the loft, it's over.

Piotr steps toward the door. "Just leave it, Jurek. There's nothing interesting in here after all. Let's go."

When the boys are outside, out of earshot, Róża exhales

and reaches for Shira's hand. She tries to think up a plan for if they return, if they wish to scale the loft. Perhaps Henryk can move the ladder away—

But Piotr is back within the hour, this time with a different boy. Róża fears the hay has shifted, that they aren't completely covered over, but she doesn't dare move. Her breath catches in her throat. Her hand, clammy with sweat, is still on Shira's.

"Did your family keep pigs in here?" the boy asks.

"I don't know what's been in here. I'm sorry it smells, but at least we can be alone."

"There's hay up there," the other boy says, pointing at the loft.

"I think it's more smelly. Over here is better."

Piotr leads the boy to the corner of the barn. Soon Róża hears the press of a body against the wall, a heaviness of breath. Heat floods the pit of her stomach. She strains to see through the hay as the boys fumble to push their pants lower, raise their shirts higher.

Róża is unsure if Shira's face is turned toward or away from the corner. Can she see what's happening? What if she makes a noise?

The barn door flies open, again catching Róża unawares— and the boys too. They split apart, but not before Krystyna sees.

"Dariusz, it's time for you to leave. Now." Krystyna's voice is shrill.

The boys scrabble with their clothes, tugging and buttoning, heads bowed, faces reddened, as they duck out of the barn.

Heart rattling, Róża watches Krystyna's face—tilted

toward the loft, questioning what the boys have witnessed, what Róża has—before she turns to go.

She listens as Krystyna follows Piotr into the farmhouse, as Dariusz pounds down the road. Shira wriggles her hand away.

"Shira?" Róża whispers, trying to unstopper her breath.

No answer.

"You did a good job staying still and silent."

"Why did Pani Wiśniewska scold like that?"

"She was frightened."

"Why?"

Róża pauses, wondering again what Shira saw. "She wants Piotr to be safe."

"Is he?"

"Yes, Shirke." But even as Róża says this, her lips form prayers for him.

That evening Krystyna and Henryk huddle by the coop. Róża can just make out Krystyna's urgent pleading.

"I want them out now."

"Has something happened?"

"No."

"Are you certain?"

"Nothing has happened. I just want them out."

"Krystyna, I don't understand—"

"It's not safe. We have to protect our own."

"You were the one who said they had no place to go."

Krystyna covers her face with her hands and turns toward the house. "I have to get back to Łukasz."

Róża scans the loft. If she'd kept even one ruby or a small bag of yeast, she'd have something to barter with at the next hiding place. In the corner, she sees Shira's blanket amid a collection of tiny hay nests, each lined with a puff of rabbit fur. She checks her pockets for the photographs, Natan's watch and compass. Her fingers brush against her mother's frosting tip.

When Henryk comes in that night, Róża again expects him to tell her they must leave the barn. She braces herself, fearing the journey to the next village, the possibility of refusal from the merchant's wife. But he does not evict them. Instead, it is the usual nightly visit.

Days later, a neighbor corners Krystyna as she is pinning clothes on the line and inquires about the boy Dariusz.

"What about him?" Krystyna asks.

"I saw him hanging around here. Was he a friend of your boys?"

"He was Piotr's classmate—" Krystyna's voice is gravel.

"Well," the neighbor keens, "he's been *taken*."

"Taken?"

She leans in closer to Krystyna, eyes glinting. "Borys turned him in. Suspected he had a contagion. You know how the Germans deal with that—"

Róża sees Krystyna's face blanch. "A contagion?" Krystyna asks limply.

"Yes. It's good he's gone from our boys."

Róża shifts and lowers herself beneath hay. For the next several hours she doesn't dare peer out at the road for fear of seeing sugar cookies piled high on plates, of hearing castrati jokes, of witnessing Piotr being dragged away.

Chapter 9

Autumn 1941

Róża wakes, cold and stiff. Since the weather turned, she has positioned herself to block Shira from the draft that presses in and embroiders the wall cracks with early morning frost. But now Shira has her pinned, and the slightest attempt to extend a leg sets her calf muscles seizing. She can't even snake an arm up to scratch her scalp—infested with lice despite constant hair braiding—lest she awaken Shira and begin even earlier the challenge of keeping her quiet through yet another day. *When will it end?* The silent counting contests and statue games get them only so far before Shira is tapping out her music, what seem like full-blown symphonies she can hardly keep contained.

Pressed against the floorboards, the hay tamped down, the back of Róża's head aches. At the point when she can't take the position any longer, she shifts a hip a little at a time, feeling Natan's no-longer-ticking watch press against her thigh. Shira doesn't wake. Gratefully, Róża drops back to sleep.

Krystyna comes in later that morning, not to take Shira out but to bring distractions. She must be a mind reader, for in a bucket she's concealed a crochet hook, yarn, pencils and paper, an atlas, and the Polish children's novel *In Desert and Wilderness* tucked inside the cover of a different title, *Emil und die Detektive.*

"They're meant to be reading only German books now." Krystyna points to the book cover. "But my boys loved this one."

Róża wants to thank Krystyna for not evicting them—today marks fifty-six days in the barn—and to tell her that she would never utter a word about Piotr, but she hesitates, fearful of causing offense or sounding as though she's using it as leverage to remain in the loft. Krystyna already contends with Henryk's grumblings over rushed chores, as she's instituted that Piotr go to church each morning.

"We are so grateful for your kindness. Thank you," Róża says.

The closest thing they've had to a book is the cardboard fold of photographs. Now Róża whisper-reads the first pages of *In Desert and Wilderness* to Shira, pausing to open the atlas to Port Said at the northern end of the Suez Canal, where this story of intrigue and adventure takes place. Shira *ahh*s with pleasure at the description of flamingos, "red and purple flowers suspended in the sky," then claps a hand to her mouth.

"I'm sorry," she whimpers. "Please, keep reading?"

"Shira," Róża whispers, "now that we have paper I want to teach you your letters. You can learn to spell your name." Róża prints out the letters of the alphabet on a sheet of paper, circling the letters in Shira's name, but Shira insists on turning the paper over on its blank side and reorienting it sideways.

"I'd like a music page."

"What?"

"A music page, with the lines across, like you and *Tata*—"
Shira closes her mouth again. Outside, the sky is white. No
birds in the branches now.

"Let's work on your letters."

Róża knows: music paper will lead to music *making*, or
at the very least to tapping. But sulking—which Shira looks
as though she is about to start—may lead to a storminess that
will be even more difficult to manage. "How about this: I'll
tell you a real-life story about some famous musicians."

"Good."

"Come onto my lap so I can whisper even more quietly. It's
about a violinist, a very talented violinist named Joachim.
He was *so* dedicated to his music, in fact, that he believed
that he and his musician friends should never marry."

"Why?"

"He thought it would distract them. He wanted them to
stay faithful to their calling as musicians. He even had a personal motto, *Frei aber einsam*—Free but lonesome."

"He wanted them to be lonesome?"

"It's not that he wanted them to be lonesome. He thought
that music would be even better company."

"Dora got a dog as a birthday gift."

"Hmm." From a neighbor's window Róża had witnessed
the roundup that took Shira's friend Dora and her family
away—this, the day before Natan didn't return home. She
stares hard at Shira, forcing a small smile. "Well, as a gift
for Joachim, his friends composed a sonata for him based
on the musical notes F-A-E, for *Frei aber einsam*. Diet-
rich wrote the first movement; Schumann wrote the second
movement; and Brahms wrote the third. A scherzo."

"I wish I could hear it."

She doesn't mention that Shira *has* heard Brahms's

Scherzo. Natan used to practice it, repeatedly and meticulously. "If you promise to be very quiet, I can hum the first bars for you. It's in minor mode, which is tricky, and it starts off very dramatically."

Though her own eyes are closed, Róża feels Shira's eyes roaming her face as she hums the beginning of the violin melody. Róża wonders if Shira composes equally exceptional music in her head.

"Mama, will you write it on the paper? I promise I'll keep it tucked in my pocket, I won't make a noise."

Chapter 10

Shira purses her lips tight so the notes won't escape. Over and over, she hums what her mother hummed for her of Brahms's Scherzo—the start, like branches rapping against a window, then a soulful, happy melody. She keeps her eyes trained on the crack in the loft wall. Pale orange light bleeds into the gray. It is just before dawn.

The first commotion of the morning comes from the birds: the *kiuks* of woodpeckers, the *krekks* of terns. At daybreak, Henryk trudges to the fields. The older boys do their chores, then Piotr departs for church. Krystyna bustles about, pulling stiff shirts from the clothesline, with Łukasz perched on her hip. Łukasz squeals when she puts him down, so she picks him up again and steps into the farmhouse, and Shira imagines him swaying amid the folds of Krystyna's skirt, pressing a hard crust against his tender new teeth.

The usual villagers canter past on their errands—the white-haired lady whose flowery housedress ruffles between her long coat and boots, the two stringy blond girls, late as always, for work.

For a long stretch of time, Shira occupies herself hiding "treasures"—bits of broken blue-and-white china she's dislodged with a stick from an earthen corner of the barn. Each shard she turns over and over in her hand, considering where she might stow it, undetected. One she snugs into the nook where a crosstie meets a rafter; another she places inside a wood knot of a floorboard. Two oblong bits that nearly fit together Shira hides along the back wall, farthest from the ladder, deep beneath hay.

Shrieks of children at play come from a nearby yard. Soon it will be time for Krystyna to bring their meal pail. Shira hopes there will be bread to dip into the weed soup and an apple each. Yesterday she nibbled her apple so slowly it lasted all afternoon, the juice of each tiny bite spraying in her mouth and onto her lips, the smell of autumn sticking to her fingers.

She halts her solitary game to peer again through the crack of the loft wall. The nearest tree branches wave their silvery undersides; the tall brown grasses tick in the breeze. Shira strains to listen for the sap flowing within the blue bark of the maples. She hopes, in vain, for Krystyna to come take her out of the barn.

Eventually Shira settles back into the hay, shifting against the sharp press of her mother's hip, inhaling her pungent odor. She wonders when Henryk will bring another bathing bucket. She enjoys the feel of the warm water, how her mother rubs the tickly cloth between her fingers and toes. One time Shira got to eat an egg outside the barn *and* have a sponge bath in the very same day. She tries to figure out, *How many days ago was that?* but her mother interrupts.

"Shirke, it's time for lessons." Her mother smooths out the

alphabet page and sets it aside. She begins on a new sheet, drawing columns. "Today we are going to learn numbers. I'd like to teach you to count all the way to fifty, because you're five years old and fifty is ten times five!"

"Am I ever going to school?"

"We have to stay here for now."

"But other kids—"

Her mother's voice is low. "If you're very quiet, we can play a letters game."

Shira wants to protest—she wishes to go outside, to go to school—but her mother's eyes, blinking hard like window shutters, close her out.

Later her mother reads from *In Desert and Wilderness*, low and close to Shira's ear, pointing to the words as she goes and encouraging Shira to sound out the smallest ones. Shira likes shaping her mouth around each sound. She is eager to learn to read, even if, with this Polish book, it feels a bit like pretending. The books on her bedside shelf at home are in Yiddish.

After a few more pages her mother puts aside the book, open winged. Circles ring the hollow of her eyes, blue black like the sky at midnight, and lines etch her mouth. Shira feels the worry in her mother's breath. She disentangles herself.

The birds outside strike up their dusk calls and Shira adjusts her gaze to watch them through the crack in the barn wall. Their eyes, glassy like the eyes of her stuffed animals, flit in every direction. Several lack digits on one foot, the left. This makes them hop somewhat crookedly and lean sideways when they perch.

A few days later, Shira hears soldiers outside the barn. They've never been so close; she's heard them by the tavern and along the road, singing, on foot and on horses, but now they stand just beneath the tree near the side of the barn wall. Are they going to enter? Shira's mother covers the waste bucket and arranges hay thickly over Shira before sliding herself down into a concealed position.

A bead of sweat trickles from Shira's hairline, causing her to shudder. The plan of where to run has changed; it's no longer to the root cellar. But *where*? She didn't pay attention when her mother told her because she'd had a song in her head. She was going to ask later, but—

"Even the birds around here are deformed," a soldier says. He circles the tree in giant steps.

Worry clenches at Shira's stomach. If they don't like the outside birds, will they dislike *hers*?

"It must be a genetic problem, unless a disease swept through the flock." This is a different soldier talking, one with a softer voice.

"Let's shoot them."

"No, I don't want—"

Shira wishes she knew the prayer her mother constantly mouthed.

"They don't *matter*. Look at them."

"We mustn't spend our bullets."

"I have plenty of spares."

When Shira hears a gun cock, she sinks lower in the hay, tears stinging her eyes. Shots fire. Wings beat frantically against the sky. Shira begins humming, a melody to drown out tragedy. When her mother hushes her with a near-silent hiss, she in turn hushes her bird, who rears and pecks, angrily, not wanting to be silenced.

Chapter 11

When Róża hears the soldiers taking shots at the birds, she thinks of Natan. *Where did they shoot him? In the back, when he was already on his knees?*

Four days in a row, soldiers had rounded up the young, able-bodied Jews of Gracja for labor duty. The men had returned each night filthy and exhausted, but Natan had felt sure that their usefulness, their hard work, was saving them. Saving *all* of them.

On the fifth day only half of the men returned. Oskar, their neighbor, shook so hard he could barely speak despite Róża's frantic pleas for information.

"You must tell me, Oskar. Where is he? Is he all right?"

"They made us dig trenches."

"But where is *Natan*? Is he still there? Are they housing some of the men closer? He is strong. Maybe they think it's good to get an early start tomorrow?"

"Róża—"

"I know, not *so* strong, but hardworking, dogged. Yes?"

"Róża, you have to listen to me."

"Why didn't he tell me to pack a bag? I could have sent him with clean clothes."

"They forced us to dig trenches."

"He told me, it was very hard work. Such deep trenches."

"They had all of us line up in front of them."

"Why they need such deep trenches, who knows, but—"

"Róża, they shot more than half of us. After we'd dug all day. I don't know why I'm here. It's not right that I am here, when Natan—" Oskar buried his face in his hands.

Róża stepped back, stunned.

She ran, legs quaking beneath her, home, where they lived together with her parents. Her father ushered Shira away; her mother held her as she railed and sobbed and eventually tucked her into bed. Róża blinked at the pale papered walls, the bedspread with yellow sunflowers, the wood-carved elephants, trunks entwined upon the bureau. This room—the room she shared with Natan—was unrecognizable to her. The world ceased to make sense.

Two days later the soldiers swept through their building and took her parents. In the shadowy darkness of the closet, clutched tight to Shira, inhaling the floury scent at the collar of her mother's camel-hair coat, she could feel Shira's eyes fixed on her, bringing to mind her own mother's face. Róża signaled to Shira to be silent and held back her own sobs as she heard the pounding of boots on the stairs, her parents' shrieks echoing in the wall. Her fingers encircled the metal frosting tip, buried deep in the pocket of her mother's coat.

Afterward, alive because an altercation down the hall had distracted the soldiers from an all-out search, Róża comprehended one single fact: They could not stay here.

She waited only for soldiers to vacate the street and for the cover of night. She satcheled photographs, coins and jewels, Natan's watch and compass and fur hat. She took Shira—yellow bird conjured from the same senselessness, cupped in her hands—and ran.

Róża watches Shira now, curled in her shadowy hiding spot, one cheek pressed against the music paper, tracing the illustration on her book's cloth cover—a lion posed regally on a high rock—outlining it with her pointing finger. Before the worst began happening in Gracja, Róża downplayed the denigrations: the yellow stars, the marks on the doors of Jewish businesses, including her mother and Aunt Syl's bakery. Róża only ever wanted Shira to feel pride in herself. Perhaps this is why she doesn't tell her outright the reason they have to hide, why they are hunted. She's not sure Shira would even understand if she tried to tell her.

The fall air nips. Dull light presses through the cracks.

At the bakery they would be preparing for the High Holidays, overrun with orders for honey cakes and apple cakes and babkas. Mrs. Blum would be asking, as she did every week, if the sponge cake was moist. Róża thinks of her friends and extended family, Aunt Syl and Uncle Jakob, Natan's young nieces and cousins.

Are any of them still alive to usher in a New Year?

Is there a synagogue still standing?

She turns her head toward the wall and listens for the birds who return to perch, slantwise, on the branches outside the barn.

Chapter 12

Winter 1942

Their breaths come out in frosted puffs. Even beneath piles of hay, the tips of Shira's ears sting with cold and her fingers and toes grow numb. When she begins to tremble, her skin clammy, Róża lies on top of her to keep her warm. Henryk sneaks in a wool blanket, a child's hat, and some gloves.

Shira nestles her covered head low against her pillow, a sack filled with peas. Through a crack in the wall, she looks at the ice-encased tree branches, longing for the cold to stop, for the sound of the birds to come back.

Her mother hums a bit of *The Snow Maiden*—an opera she's explained is about how winter must die for spring to come. But spring seems so far off.

"Mama, what about Brahms's Scherzo? You said you'd teach me."

Róża misses a beat as she remembers how Natan rehearsed Brahms's Scherzo with Władysław, a most talented pianist and friend. They worked it over measure by measure as other friends meandered in and out of the music room, dunking slices of her mother's mandelbrot into glasses of tea. Róża shuts her eyes and presses her cheek to her shoulder, striking the same deep-angled pose Natan struck, the whole left side of his face nuzzled against his violin as he played. In this way she recalls the stormy cascade at the beginning of the piece, the lyrical movement in the middle. She hums it for Shira once again.

Shira remains subdued even as Róża describes the bouncy bow strokes, the quick-tied notes. Is she lethargic from hunger? A broken spirit? Gauntness sucks at her once-round cheeks. Their food pail is at its most meager: a few turnips, a watery potato soup. According to the nicks in the rafter, today marks their one hundred and sixty-eighth day. Shira's quiet listlessness brings forth in Róża a collision of gratitude and despair.

"Shira"—Róża's voice strains to be cheery—"why don't we look together at the atlas?"

Only the slimmest shaft of winter's hard-edged light cuts into the barn. Róża thinks, *At least this weather may keep the Germans at bay.* She fumbles with gloved hands to turn the pages, one by one, as they look first at continents, then at countries. That the topography is *colored*— mountain ranges in pale brown, forests in green, oceans in sea blue—pleases Róża immensely.

"Do you see Vienna, there in northeastern Austria? It has the most wonderful concert hall, the Musikverein."

"Have you ever been to it?"

"No."

"Has Grandpa?"

"No—"

Róża is just about to promise Shira, to say that she'll take her there, and maybe even to Milan, to the famous opera house in Italy. But Henryk's firm slam of the farmhouse door drives Róża to swallow her words, to motion Shira to hide.

Chapter 13

Late night. Róża hopes that Shira has turned away, buried herself beneath the hay with her eyes closed as Róża has told her, so many times, to do. Henryk's boots crunch along the walkway at the far side of the barn. Róża pulls hastily at the tangles in her hair and swallows hard, trying to clear her breath.

When Henryk ascends the ladder, he pulls a wrapped-up potato from his pocket, and for several minutes he is all patience, stretching out on his side, leaning on one bent elbow, watching Róża as she takes a bite of it and stows the rest for Shira. He smells of animals and wood smoke, and his dark eyes train on her, horselike. He produces another gift: an extra pair of socks. Róża nods her gratitude and Henryk reaches out gently to touch her hair.

He takes his time unbuttoning her shirt, untying the rope around her waist, shimmying her pants over her narrow hips and buttocks. He does not touch her, not yet. He props himself beside her and looks at her for a long while. As his eyes move over her, Róża turns her face toward the wall, jaw clenched. Shivering.

Henryk puts a finger to her cheek and rotates her face back toward him. His eyes, full of intensity, lock on hers. Róża feels an involuntary flap in her belly, a pulsing heat below. She finds it uncomfortable but also exhilarating to be looked at like this, to be seen, after so much hiding.

Henryk takes Róża quickly then. She wants to be numb to him—she holds still, moving neither with him nor against him, Shira just a few feet away.

When it's over she ventures, "The next days are a fertile time."

"What are you saying?"

"I'm saying, it's risky. You don't always pull out quickly and—"

"You're telling *me* what's risky?" His breath is hot at her neck. His hard slap stings her cheek.

When he is gone, down the ladder two rungs at a time and out of the barn, Róża turns her head to look at Shira. Her eyes are closed and she is breathing evenly, asleep. Slowly, soundlessly, Róża pads down the ladder and squeezes through a small opening in the barn door. The air is frigid and snow covers the ground, but she needs this moment outside.

There are no lights on in the house. Róża wonders, *Is Krystyna asleep or awake? Could she be relieved that I take Henryk's attentions?* Her thoughts circle continuously around the two of them, trying to make sense of their relationship. Henryk has his ulterior motives, but Krystyna is truly pious, Róża thinks—and generous. She should be grateful for the eggs she gives Shira to eat.

Róża steps around the side of the barn, pulls down her pants, and squats to pee. It burns where she's been chafed.

She takes a handful of snow and wipes between her legs, a cold, wet salve, before pulling her pants back on. She cradles her bruised elbows, roughed up by the floorboards, and returns to the barn. She scales the ladder and, still stinging, retreats into the hay.

She wants Natan so desperately in this moment. His lips blanketing her in kisses, causing her to quiver with desire like a taut string. They might have shared the same pulse, the same knocking heartbeat, their love as raw and intense as, now, her heartache.

Róża lifts Shira on top of her, needing the feel of her girl's body upon hers. Shira's hair has slipped out of its braid and feathers against Róża's face. Róża inhales deeply, wishing to dispel the smell of wet, smoky wool Henryk has left on her. For a fleeting moment, Róża imagines that Shira is the mother and she is the child. She folds her palm over Shira's outstretched hand and holds on tight.

It is late afternoon when Shira searches the hay, frantic. She bats at her eyes to keep tears from welling up.

"What are you looking for, Shira?" her mother whispers.

"Mama, I can't find my bird—I think he's at the Wiśniewskis'!"

Shira doesn't tell her mother that her bird prefers being outside, where it's fresh and light and there are treats to eat. Still, Shira was firm that he needed to stay in the barn, hidden—no chirping or even stretching his wings—but he slipped out when Shira went with Krystyna, and now he's stalling his return.

Shira's stuffed belly is in rebellion again, full of regret. She didn't bring any food back for her mother. She had stinky diarrhea in the straw basin, causing a terrible smell in the loft; and now she fears her bird will never come back to her. She paces the loft, forgetting to be silent and still.

"Come, now. He'll find his way back." Róża covers the basin with hay to mask the smell until Henryk can move it out to the animal pen.

"No, he won't and it's all my fault!" Tears stream down Shira's cheeks. She drops to the loft floor and begins pounding on the boards.

Her mother grabs hold of Shira, pins her arms against her chest. "*Nie!* Quiet this instant."

The notes in her mother's voice are cold and harsh. Shira struggles against the hold.

In this moment, she doesn't care that it isn't completely dark, that it isn't safe for her mother outside. At nightfall, her mother is going to shunt her off to the far wall, and Shira will have to shut her eyes and plug her ears even when it sounds like Henryk is hurting her mother. She can't do that without her bird!

She begs in an urgent whisper, "Will you go get him? He can't spend the night in the farmhouse."

"Shh. Stop your silliness."

"Please, Mama!"

Her mother makes a frustrated huffing sound, but she descends the ladder. She disappears beneath the loft, then reappears with one hand cupped and hoists herself single-handed back up.

How could she get him so quickly?

Shira inspects the bird, suspicious that it is another one, not hers. But she sees that it *is* hers, by the tiny white spot on his beak and by the single feather that is always ruffled, refusing to tuck in. Shira holds him to her chest. His heart beats fast like marching boots, like gunshots. When she tries to pat him, he ducks and flaps as if to say he won't be so easily soothed.

Shira turns her back to her mother as she cuddles her bird close, murmuring, "I need you with me always."

Something in the way Shira turns away, cooing to her bird, sends Róża into a spinning rage. In the face of all that Róża does—she gives Shira most of every meal (this, despite the eggs Krystyna gives to Shira and never to her!); she encourages Shira's musical interest even when it reminds her painfully of Natan; she soothes her with lullabies, invents elaborate stories to entertain her and pass the time—yet still Shira pushes the limits, wishing for walks with Krystyna and fussing over her bird, risking the safety of *both* of them, *all* of them. Is she so nervy now as to be modeling "motherly care"?

Her chest draws tight, full of fury. But after an hour sitting in the stale, shadowy blackness—nowhere to go—inhaling the dank smells and watching Shira clutch the empty air, her anger gutters and guilt floods in.

They've lost every real thing except each other. Must her girl fear losing even what is imaginary?

When Shira wakes the next morning, she finds her mother propped against the loft's far wall where thin shafts of sunlight stripe the barn. Her mother has the hook and yarn Krystyna gave them and she looks to be crocheting something very small, her fingers up close to her face and her eyes squinting.

"What are you making?" Shira whispers.

"You'll have to wait and see."

Relieved to hear a playful tone in her mother's voice, Shira covers her eyes with her hands. Her legs wriggle and she shifts side to side with anticipation.

At her last birthday party, a picnic by the Narew River, Shira covered her eyes while her grandmother brought out the cake. Everything seemed to smell better with her eyes covered: the sweetness of the frosting, the match's flame, the waxiness of the candles. Shira opened her eyes when she heard her mother's cello sound out the first deep notes of the birthday song, and she couldn't believe what she saw: the cake had three tiers, like a fairy castle. It had delicate loops of white piping, with five pink candles for her and twenty-five white candles for her mother—because they were born twenty years (and two days) apart. Some of Shira's friends thought Shira should have her own party, but she loved sharing it with her mama. As soon as one year's party was over, they'd set to planning the next.

"There, now you can look," her mother says, yarn still laced between her fingers.

Shira leans in to see the tiniest hat (her mother must have sized it to fit her fingertip) and a thin scarf, just three stitches wide and ten stitches long. She looks at her mother, unsure.

"They are for your bird."

"Oh, thank you, Mama."

Her mother isn't mad at her for yesterday! Shira takes the tiny clothes in her hands. Carefully, she drapes the scarf around the bird's nape and places the hat on top of its crested head.

Her mother crochets other articles of clothing: bird earmuffs (two of the tiniest granny circles connected by a strand) and a beak cover. "Because it's gotten so cold."

Shira loves it when her mother is silly.

"And here's something elegant for him to wear to the symphony," her mother says as she hands Shira a little cape.

"Mama? On the night of the concert, will we have a fancy dinner?" Shira remembers the night when, with her father's help, she accompanied her mother in a "grand concert duet" and afterward they ate a delicious roast—but she doesn't say this.

"Yes, Shirke, and we'll set pretty flowers at the table."

"Daisies?"

"And bright red poppies too."

The skin on the underside of her mother's arms is mottled bluish pink, a pattern that makes Shira think of the wallpaper in her grandmother's dressing closet.

"The girl and her mother should grow poppies in their silent garden," Shira suggests.

"Perhaps their enchanted bird will carry seeds over from the field so that they can. We'll have to wait and see."

Shira nestles with her mother, fingering the tiny bird clothes.

In each square of the quilt covering her bed in Gracja, six dainty red flowers fan out from a single stem, their leaves bowed beneath like a lyre, and two birds stand face-to-face, so close that one need not even chirp for the other to know her song.

Chapter 14

Róża paces the barn, biting down on her tongue to keep from moaning. She'd asked Henryk for the wild carrot seed as a precaution because, in addition to her stopped menses, she'd felt tender in her breasts. Now she is bleeding and the pain is excruciating. She peers out a wall crack, gauging the brightness of the night's moon.

"Mama?"

"I'm all right. I . . . just have . . . a bellyache."

Róża leans one way; another. She tries to sit, but the cramping in her womb wrenches her back to standing. She has stuffed her pants with a spare piece of cloth. It is soaked through.

"Are you hurt, Mama?"

Worry shows in the contours of Shira's face.

The quickest flash of a wish—that Shira was gone, not needing comfort, not witnessing her like this—shuttles through Róża before she works her features into a reassuring expression and faces her girl.

"I need fresh air. It's late and I need you to stay very quiet. Still as a mouse beneath the hay—you hear me?"

"Yes, *Mamusia*."

"I don't want you to move. And no calling out. Please."
With a sharp intake of breath, Róża propels one foot, then
the other, down the ladder and out the door.

In the snow, Róża bleeds red black upon the white ground,
in clumps and clots. As many times as she bears down, more
slips out; it smells like rust and metal and rot. She grows
dizzy and hot despite the frigid air. She reaches for a handful of clean snow to pat on her forehead and the back of her
neck.

Róża knows she needs to get this out of her, get herself
back inside. But beyond the pain, she wonders, *How far
along?* and, *Was it a girl or a boy?* She trains her eyes on
the far-off trees as her legs quake beneath her. With every
cramping gush, she feels a deep sorrow mingled with relief.

When the bleeding subsides, Róża lets herself sit, bare
bottomed, drained out, blinking up at the stars. One minute. Two. Fleeting moments in which to wonder, would they
have been better off back in Gracja? The remaining Jews
lived in a ghetto now, Henryk told her. If her uncle Jakob
was still there, he'd have clout, and her aunt Syl, so long
as she could get hold of the ingredients, would make bread
for them to eat. One thing's for certain: Róża wouldn't be
miscarrying, alone outside in the dead of winter. But then
she thinks of what the soldiers did to Natan in the work
fields, how they came for her parents; their thumps and
shrieks sounding through the closet door—

Róża shivers as flecks of snow drift off the barn roof. In
the moonlight, the frosted fields are a rolling silvery sheet.
Róża hoists herself up and fastens her pants after tucking another not-so-clean cloth between her legs.

She has to hide the blood before it can be discovered. Best would be to bury it away from the sight of humans and the smell of animals, but the ground is frozen and anyway she hasn't the time to dig a hole. If only she had bled into a bucket, she could have figured out a way to hide it inside the barn.

She staggers to the barn now and notices one of the small rabbits in the corner. In a quick singular motion, she swipes it up and holds it tight under her arm, feeling the rapid beat of its frantic, trapped heart. She reaches with her free arm for the trowel, pegged up on the wall. She fears Shira will start up with questions, but mercifully Shira is silent, still beneath the hay. Róża steps back outside and brings the trowel blade down upon the rabbit in a single terrible whack. The rabbit slumps, lifeless. Róża uses the blade to tear it apart the way a wolf might. At any other time, she would have regretted the waste of meat. Now the rangy smell, raw and rusty, makes her gag. Shaking, she places the torn-up rabbit on the heap of her own blood. In a vain last measure, she hacks at the ground, once, twice, hoping to loosen a bit of earth for cover, but there is no give. She mouths a prayer as she wipes her hands in the snow to clean off the blood—the rabbit's, her own—and weaves her way back into the barn, up to the loft, to Shira.

The following day, through a crack at the far edge of the loft, Róża sees Jurek poke at the mangled rabbit with a stick. At the sight of it, a frozen rusted mass, Róża heaves bile into the hay. Sweat breaks at her brow. Her womb seizes anew. Yet she focuses her eyes outside. Jurek is holding the rabbit aloft now, calling out for his father.

Henryk is there in an instant.

"If there is a fox coming around, we'll need to reinforce the coops," Jurek says, inspecting the carcass. "But it doesn't make sense that a fox would leave this meat. What else might have killed it?"

"I don't know."

"Do you think Mama would want to put it in her soup?"

Henryk's "No" comes out edged with panic.

If Krystyna inspects the scene, so close to the barn, she'll know. When Henryk speaks again, his voice is composed. "We can't know how long it's been dead. It may be unsafe to eat."

Jurek lets the rabbit drop and turns his stick to the clumps of reddened, viscid snow. "There's more blood here than could have come from one rabbit."

Shira, who has been slouched against the wall weaving hay into squares, sits upright at Jurek's mention of the word "rabbit" and begins scanning the loft and lower barn. Róża puts a finger to her sour lips.

"We've had so little meat, I really think Mama will want—"

"What she will want is for you to finish mucking out the coop. Now. I'm going to bury this so it doesn't attract other animals." Henryk retrieves a shovel from the barn without a glance loftward and starts hacking at the frozen earth.

When Henryk mounts the loft that night, Róża huddles in the corner, knees to chest, as if there were something still inside her she might be able to protect.

"Krystyna will notice that a rabbit is missing. They're to be our food."

"I'll say it escaped. I didn't know what else to do—"

Henryk touches Róża's leg. She shudders. "Don't touch me now. Please—"

His eyes darken. He slaps the floor with his hand and bounds out of the barn, leaving Shira jolted awake and Róża cowering.

Chapter 15

Spring 1942

Shira ignores her mother's frown and scurries down the ladder to greet Krystyna, who has entered the barn with a food pail. Shira is eager to eat, but she's even more excited to talk to Krystyna.

"I—I saw Łukasz take his first steps—I saw through the crack!"

"Shh!" her mother hisses from the loft.

Shira funnels her voice into a whisper. "I *saw* him. He walked."

"Yes! He's sleeping now, after his big morning," Krystyna says.

"Five whole paces!"

"Was it five?" Krystyna smiles, charmed.

"Yes—five! The grass cushioned his fall."

Róża says they are not family, but Shira feels they are. Even if Shira has to hide away when Henryk comes to the loft. Even if the boys don't actually know she's there. From her perch, she has learned that Piotr's favorite game is *zośka* and that Jurek hates mucking out the chicken coop more than any other chore. She has overheard both boys complaining about the lack of food; the menacing soldiers; how the other kids look down on their father for not fighting in the war.

Shira senses when the boys feel afraid, though the adults' fear is worse: lodged in their faces and bodies, trapped in the sounds beneath their words. Outside, when a neighbor stops by for a chat, when Krystyna excuses herself to tend to the boys and Henryk to the animals, when at night her mother asks Henryk for the latest news, Shira hears it shuttling between their whispers. She knows it from before, from when they still lived in Gracja; her parents tried with their instruments to play over it, to play through it, yet it clung to their notes anyway.

Confined within the barn, her mother invents ever more elaborate stories: To keep silence in the enchanted garden, the little girl fashions handkerchiefs out of daisy petals to muffle the princess's sneezes. She tricks the giants (whose thundering footsteps keep the flowers from blooming) by flipping the soles of their shoes so that they walk *away* from the garden rather than toward it. And with the help of her mother and her yellow bird, the little girl plants a secret strawberry patch, hidden among the sunflowers, so they'll have delicious treats that even raiders won't be able to find when they come to pillage.

Shira asks if there are any cats in the garden. The last time Krystyna took Shira out, the tabby whooshed its tail against Shira's legs, then flopped to the ground in front of her. She thought he wanted a pat, but when she knelt down and extended her hand, he tried to scratch her.

"No, there are no cats in the garden."

"Good, because they might not be nice to birds."

"The garden is safe for birds and for quiet girls."

Her mother reads to her from their one borrowed book, over and over, as Shira wants. By now Shira can sight-read small, common words—"the" and "it" and "who"—and the names of the characters "Stas" and "Nell." And her mother has permitted Shira to use five whole sheets of paper for music lines rather than for letters and numbers. She makes plans for when they will leave the barn, hums bits of Brahms's Scherzo and the nightly lullaby, whispers even when her body hurts, which Shira knows from the way her mother's mouth pouches, as if stuffed with an imaginary sponge, her teeth barely touching down. The words pile up so as to chase away pain, to topple fear, to prove that they, alone, are family enough.

Yet Shira still longs for her *tata*, her grandparents, her friends, her home. She stares at the photographs, lingering longest on the picture of herself, fancy in her ankle-length dress—a night they were all together. She nestles her bird and awaits Krystyna's visits. She stays glued to the crack in the wall, listening for the boys' conversations, watching as Łukasz toddles forward and reaches for Jurek's and Piotr's open hands.

Chapter 16

Rumors swirl of denunciations and shootings and a burned-down barn the next village over. Henryk digs a hole in the barn floor that he conceals with a hay bale, so Róża and Shira can move to a different hiding space without leaving the barn. He spreads the surplus dirt on the barn floor and carries the rest in buckets out to the fields.

Later, up in the loft, Henryk caresses Róża's cheek before he undresses her. He's been gentler since the miscarriage, since that one time she'd asked not to be touched.

Still, Róża's voice shakes as she asks, "You'll pull out quickly?" She *can't* get pregnant again.

"Yes."

Róża continues to lie mostly still while Henryk is with her. Yet, the way her body responds to him changes. She tells herself that it is involuntary when her nipples knot, when she goes slick. Their bodies know each other now.

She wants to remember her time with Natan, their courtship, their first tender kisses. But if she's honest, he's gone blurry in her mind. It is the hunger, she's sure of it, and the unrelenting stress. Even with her eyes closed to reality, it is

Henryk's form that closes in. He does things to her that he mustn't do to Krystyna—things Natan would never have dreamed of—and her body responds.

Róża tells herself: She and Shira are alive because of this. She tells herself: Even if Shira has to lie just a few strides away, her ears buzzing with the press of sex, Róża is doing what she needs to do. She tells herself: She is keeping them safe.

Shira's mother is always ordering her to be still and silent, but then Henryk mounts the loft ladder, and *he* moves around and makes terrible noises. Her mother doesn't say anything, and she forbids Shira even from turning her head or opening her eyes. She just has to lie there, frightened, listening to Henryk's bumping and gasping and what sounds like strangled screaming.

It is hot beneath the hay, and Shira labors to breathe. She wishes her *tata* were here to make it stop. On her own, there's nothing to do but to wait. Drown out the sounds with the music she hears in her head, dark and foreboding.

When Henryk finally climbs down the ladder and leaves the barn, Shira steals a look at her mother, staring up at the ceiling, panting. It's the only time Shira can't read her mother's face.

Chapter 17

As the weather warms, the barn sweats. The hay, dry and sweet scented in winter, grows dank in the loft. Moisture gathers in the rafters and the wallboards expand. The cracks shrink to reveal less of the farmhouse, less of the road.

Still, the *sound* of the boys floats up to the loft; Shira can hear Jurek and Piotr bicker as they pound a rickety fence post back into position.

Shira's mother grows cross when the boys are about. She hunches against the wall, her arms folded across her chest, wishing to block out their voices. But Shira hangs on their conversations.

They used to complain about having to go to school, but now that it's been closed, Piotr wants it to reopen.

"Maybe farm life is fine for *you*," Piotr says.

"I like it all right." Jurek's words come out in the rhythm of his hammer swings.

"Well, I want to train to become a doctor."

"You'll have to go to school forever. It's not worth it."

"It *is* worth it. And it's not right that I can't have the chance—"

Shira licks the remnants of Krystyna's cauliflower soup, then puts the pail aside. Her bird ruffles his wings, hops across her crossed legs, and pecks at her shoes.

"Shh," she whispers. "I told you, you have to stay still and silent. You have to *hide*."

The bird's eyes are full of questions, so she continues: "Birds like you are not allowed to be out, not allowed to fly."

Shira knows he doesn't understand. She wishes she had better answers. Even the girl in the enchanted garden doesn't really know what's happened to her *tata* or the rest of her family, or why others can make sounds but she needs to be silent and hide. Sometimes her mother mutters about being different, about having pride in who she is, but it doesn't make any sense!

Outside, a stork burrows into its nest atop the neighbor's potato *ziemianka*.

"You are different. I don't know how, exactly; you just are. Stay down, I said. Shh!"

In the loft late at night, Henryk's hands tremble and his spooked eyes dart as he describes what he's heard: The burned-down barn belonged to a farmer who was seen giving food to a family of Jews crossing into the woods. German soldiers strung him to the crossbeam before lighting the fire.

Róża looks away.

For a week, only Henryk enters the barn. Instead of pails containing Krystyna's soups or stews, he ferries large wooden boxes with stray potatoes and a water canteen rattling beneath farm tools. Róża wonders if Krystyna is lobbying for them to leave; if Henryk is the one now petitioning for them to stay.

Just once in the course of the week Henryk reaches for Róża. She reaches back.

Chapter 18

Summer 1942

When Shira begins coughing, all Róża can focus on is the sound of it, who might hear: The boys? A neighbor on the way to the tavern? A soldier? *God help us.*

She props Shira up and holds her close, more to muffle than to soothe her, and she nearly smothers her when Henryk or Krystyna comes into the barn.

The coughing persists. Róża tries, gently and not so gently, to shush her. She needs it to stop.

"Hush, Shira. Please."

By nightfall, the third night, the coughing stops. Róża says a prayer of thanks. But soon she realizes Shira's condition is *worse*. Her cheeks glow red; she shudders with chills yet radiates heat. Come morning, her eyes are glassy and she is lethargic.

Why hadn't she realized how sick Shira was? Róża moves the damp hair off her face, hoists her into her lap. If it's typhus, they'll die together.

Henryk places water just inside the barn door and glances up. Róża sees in his expression that he knows Shira has something bad.

"I fear it's pneumonia." She doesn't dare mention her other fear. If Henryk and Krystyna thought Shira had typhus, they'd expel them at once.

"We don't have any medicine."

"Could you possibly bring me water to bathe her with and some cups?"

"Cups?"

"Small glass cups. And matches. Also, a bit of alcohol, and cotton."

"Róża—"

"I can't think what else to do. She struggles to breathe."

Róża's aunt once described the process to her: setting a flame inside a glass cup creates an air vacuum, and the cup suctions to the skin. This loosens things, makes breathing easier.

At nightfall, Henryk comes in with a box of supplies. Several rags drape over one side.

"In case she yells." He says this in a whisper. Shira doesn't hear, or else she is too dazed to care. She looks to be staring through the wall.

"Will you stay and help me?" Róża asks.

"To make sure you don't burn the barn down?"

"For that, you have the Germans."

The glasses clink as Henryk pulls them from the box. Shira doesn't turn.

"Shira?" Róża fears she is slipping by the minute. *Can she even hear?*

To Henryk she says, "There can't be any alcohol left in the cup or else it will burn her. The glass itself will be hot, so—"

"Róża, I don't think this is safe."

"Pneumonia is not safe. A high fever is not safe."

She pulls at Shira's shoulders, attempting to turn her over. "I need you to lie on your stomach, Shira. That's it, face turned to the side. Now, we're just going to cover your mouth to keep you from making a noise."

Shira accepts the gag, and the raising of her dress, without a fuss. Her compliance nearly breaks Róża.

"We are going to stick cups to your back. They're going to make you feel better."

Henryk quickly pins blankets to the loft walls to keep the match light's flare from showing outside the barn. Then, with a gloved hand, he grips one of the glasses. He pours a splash of vodka and swivels it, attempting to coat the inside of the glass. Róża clamps hold of a cotton ball with a wrench, lights it on fire, then swirls it in the glass. The alcohol flames. Before they can do anything, figure out how to place the cup on Shira's back, it shatters.

Róża struggles to breathe now, her resolve in bits.

"Maybe it is too dangerous," Henryk says.

Róża moves aside the shards of glass that landed nearest Shira, then leans her cheek in to touch her forehead, oven hot. If they can't make this work, what is going to happen to her?

Henryk reads her thoughts. He puts an arm on her shoulder. "We'll try once more."

He prepares the second glass and Róża holds a flaming cotton ball inside it. It burns and flares, and the glass darkens to the rim, but it doesn't shatter. As the flame winks out, Henryk passes the glass to Róża, gloved hand to gloved hand.

She looks at Henryk, who looks back at her, uncertain. Shira's expression is blank. Róża feels feverish herself, dizzy and hot, but she takes a breath and places the cup on Shira's back. Shira stiffens only slightly.

Is Róża burning her, yet she is too torpid to react?

"I'm sorry, Shirke. I'm trying to make you well." She moves the cup in a circular motion until it suctions tight to one spot. "Do you think you can handle two more?"

Shira blinks.

Shira falls asleep with three glasses stuck to her back. Róża does not know how long they are supposed to stay on, so after a few more minutes she wrestles a finger beneath each rim to break the suction and pulls them off. Shira's skin is welted, red, and angry, but she sleeps on.

Henryk uses his sleeved arm to sweep the shattered glass into the box.

"I'm sorry we broke that one." Róża wraps the three intact glasses in rags and places them by Henryk's legs.

"I hope Shira will get well."

Róża sees the uncertainty still in his eyes.

By morning, Shira's rattled wheezes give way to smoother, less jagged breaths. Her forehead is sticky with sweat. She awakens late in the day, still flushed but clear-eyed and focused. Róża floods with relief when, at nightfall, Shira asks her to hum a lullaby.

Her back has three rounded welts, bruises circling the edges.

As Shira recuperates, Róża skips her usual lessons on words, sums, and maps and instead teaches Shira about music. She starts by drawing two staffs, each with five lines and four spaces, and explains how the lower-pitched notes sit on the lower part of the staff and the higher-pitched notes sit higher.

She draws a treble clef on the top staff and a bass clef on the bottom.

"What are those for?"

"They tell you where to place your notes on the staff."

"Why are they different?"

"They're for writing music for different instruments."

"Why?" Shira's stare doesn't veer from the page.

"Different instruments have different pitch ranges. It would be impossible to fit them into a staff with just one clef."

"Which is used for violin music?"

"The treble clef. You know how the violin can go very high, while the cello can go very low?"

Shira takes the pencil and tries over and over to draw a treble clef.

"I can't do it."

"It takes practice. The treble clef tells you that the note G appears on the second line, like this." Róża writes the G note into the treble staff, then places the other notes around it. "Now look at how it is for the bass clef, where much of the music for cello is written. The F note appears on the *fourth* line."

When Róża writes notes into the bass staff, she varies them, using wholes, halves, quarters, and eighths.

"What are those?"

"They're all notes, but they last for different lengths of time."

"Why?"

Shira never asks this many questions about places on the map!

"Sometimes you want the notes to be long and continuous and sometimes you want them to be short and quick, right?"

Shira nods.

Róża takes some strands of hay. She keeps one long strand intact and breaks others. She illustrates the value of notes this way: the long strand is a whole note; two half-size strands represent half notes; four quarter-size strands represent quarter notes. "I'm sorry, I can't tear the hay small enough to show you the eighths!"

Shira rummages in the hay and pulls out the paper with the beginning of Brahms's Scherzo on it. Róża can see, she is examining it anew. There's still so much to explain— the flats, the ties—but Shira looks tired. She'll teach her more tomorrow.

Róża writes out the musical notes to a simpler piece: their nightly lullaby.

> *Cucuricoo!*
> *Di mom iz nisht do.*
> *Vu hat zi geyn?*
> *Tzu bakumen a glaz fun tay.*
> *Vas is gegangen tsu trinken es?*
> *Mir aun dir.*

The tune repeats, gentle and lilting, like a boat crisscrossing a placid lake. For the rest of the afternoon, Shira hums it quietly, contentedly, over and over, pointing at it note by note as she goes.

At first, Shira does not understand how her mother's marks on the music page match the sounds of their lullaby, but then something snaps into place and Shira sees how the pattern of notes matches the swaying melody, the simple rhythmic repeats. She turns once again to the start of Brahms's

Scherzo, and what has looked like her mother's scribbles co-alesces into the repeat crescendo of staccato notes, sounds she remembers from her mother's humming, her father's practice sessions. A new feverish feeling, this one from ex-citement and urgency, washes over her. The concertos her parents played, the symphonies her grandfather listened to, the music that rushes through her own head, can be put onto paper! Shira can write all of it into these staffs—even the feelings embedded within. She reaches for a pencil.

Chapter 19

On a cool September day, frantic screams pierce the silence of the barn. Peering through a crack, Róża sees Krystyna shooing a pig out of the root cellar. Next: the pig darting around the front of the barn, squealing.

"What is it, Mama?"

"Shh. A pig got loose."

From the despair in Krystyna's shouts, Róża guesses the pig feasted on the winter store. Róża had watched as the family stockpiled the harvest and stowed it in the cellar, hoping to avoid a German raid. It seems the pig sniffed it out.

Róża thinks: *This* could be what finally exiles her and Shira from the barn. Krystyna will no longer have enough to feed her family, plus two. Róża hoists herself, weak and stiff, to standing; then she sees the barn door shifting open. She ducks beneath the hay, grabbing Shira with her. She squeezes Shira's wrist tight, a code for utter silence.

Jurek's high-pitched pig calls trail up. "Pigpigpigpig! Where are you hiding?" He seems to be circling beneath the loft.

Within her hay burrow, Róża holds her breath, then swallows, trying to stifle the heaving. Henryk bursts in just then.

"Jurek, come out of there."

"But *Tata*, the pig—"

"This instant." His voice carries a note of fear.

Róża keeps hold of Shira's wrist long after the barn door closes. She insists they remain buried until dark. Shira grows restless and tries to wriggle her hand away, but Róża doesn't let go. Their bellies growl. Krystyna does not arrive with soup. Henryk does not visit either.

Eventually Róża unwraps half of an old potato she's saved and gives it to Shira. Shira eats it and afterward sucks on a small pebble to keep her mouth occupied.

"Mama, tell me again why are we hiding from Jurek?"

"Because he might tell someone we are here."

"Who?"

"I don't know. A past schoolmate. A neighbor. It's too dangerous."

"The Wiśniewskis know we're here."

"They are helping to keep us safe."

"But Mama . . . ?"

Róża doesn't answer immediately. She listens to the gathering night, wonders if there is a chance Henryk will come. "Hmm?"

"What did we do wrong?"

"We didn't do anything wrong, Shira. It's very difficult to explain—"

"Did they get the pig back into the pen?"

"Yes."

"I want to go home."

Weak with hunger, Róża drifts off to sleep. She wakes to find Shira hunched over the pad of paper, scribbling on a new sheet. Shira has managed to draw staffs, crooked and uneven but legible, with symbols resembling the treble clef on some and the bass clef on others. Except for the last, all the staffs are filled with notes.

"What have you got there?"

"My music."

"You are writing it, just from what I told you? I need to tell you about key signatures and rests and—" A sideways glance at the paper and Róża can see: two lyrical melodies, intricately entwined. Astonishment catches in her throat. The tunes Shira hums have always been advanced, but this composition is another level entirely. Is her child a prodigy?

"I am writing a violin part and a cello part. You could play it with *Ta*—" Shira looks up, worried.

Róża turns away but manages to say, "It's brilliant, Shirke. Maybe *you'll* learn the violin one day and we'll play it together."

Krystyna comes to the barn before dawn. Róża fears she'll take stock of the rabbits, but her eyes are focused on Shira. "Is she asleep?"

Róża nods.

"I think you should move her."

"What?"

"For her safety. I know someone who is part of a network that hides children. Shira will be better off in a convent orphanage than in this barn."

Róża jolts to a stand, her legs tangling in hay as she takes a step backward, her thoughts ringing in protest: *Absolutely not; I will never part with my girl.*

She hovers over Shira now to see if she's woken her. No. She struggles to breathe.

Róża is aware that the risks here have become too much

to bear. The food supply is low. And Krystyna *surely* knows about Henryk's visits. She must see him duck into the barn on his way back from the tavern.

Róża combs the loft for their few possessions. She will collect Shira and get out now. To where she does not know, only that it will be best for her and Krystyna both. The nicks in the rafter top four hundred and sixty—more than she could have ever hoped for.

"I realize how much danger we've put you in. I am sorry," Róża says. She has seen Krystyna, her arms tight around Łukasz's shoulders, ushering him away from the barn.

"Róża, it's for *her* sake. The nuns will see to it that she gets exercise and schooling. She'll be far safer hidden among the devout."

Róża stops moving and stares hard at Krystyna. She has a kind face, deerlike. The curled blond hairs at the nape of her neck, too short to be swept into her high bun, puff around her face like soft cotton. Is it her faith in her Christian God that drives Krystyna to make such an offer? Or an emotional attachment to Shira? Perhaps she's dreamed of having a little girl. Could Krystyna be right, that Shira would be safer apart from Róża?

Róża thinks of how treacherous the journey *here* had been, with Shira constantly needing to be carried and soothed, quieted and fed. She recalls crossing the long stretch of pasture. She'd *needed* Shira to walk on her own, but Shira kept kicking off her shoes and reaching for Róża to pick her up. Over and over, Shira complained that her *tata* would have carried her. Róża dragged her in her stocking feet until Shira pleaded, promised to wear her shoes and walk—

"You can arrange for this?"

"As I told you, I know someone who does this work. My sister, actually."

Róża drops to her knees, disconcerted, as the trust she's placed in Krystyna clouds with doubt. *Her* sister *knows of our hiding? What guarantee is there that she will keep Shira safe?*

Instinctively, Róża's fingers go to where her wedding ring used to be. She looks around the tight space of the loft. It has been exhausting to keep Shira hushed up, day and night.

"Your sister—she would accompany Shira to a convent?"

"Yes."

"Why do you help us so?" Róża blurts.

Krystyna's motivations continue to confound Róża. Might she *like* separating Róża from her girl, a way of punishing her for Henryk's attentions?

Krystyna looks squarely at Róża. "In God's eyes your child is no different than mine. She deserves every chance to live."

Róża looks away, chastened.

Chapter 20

Autumn 1942

Before Róża and Krystyna settle on a plan, Germans sweep into the village. Some by horse. Some by car. They teem the area. For three days, neither Krystyna nor Henryk enters the barn. Róża and Shira stay buried deep in hay, foggy from hunger, silent, and unmoving. The tavern emits a raucous din long into the night. Shira falls in and out of sleep, but Róża remains awake, vigilant. Her parched throat itches from hay dust; her skin goes clammy from the sweat that dries cold.

When she hears what sounds like an approach on the farmhouse, Róża shuttles Shira down the ladder. Shira has been terrified to get into the narrow dugout that Henryk made in the barn floor, but now there is no choice. Róża moves the hay bale that covers the opening and hustles them into the hole. Dirt loosens and slips with her every movement. It's cold and dank and, when Róża pulls the bale back over the top, completely dark.

They shiver and blink, and suddenly it occurs to Róża that there are objects in the loft, unconcealed, that might give them away. The atlas. The novel. If pressed, Henryk can say that his boys like to read up there. But what about the other things? The needle and thread. The alphabet pages— Jurek and Piotr are too old and Łukasz too young for them. And the music pages—no one in Henryk's family plays an instrument. How can Henryk possibly explain these things? Far worse is the waste pail, which surely smells terrible after so many days. Neither he nor Krystyna could come to remove it, and in her haste Róża didn't think to cover it. Henryk no longer has the excuse of his livestock animals— they've killed them all for meat. The straying pig was the last to go.

There's nothing to do. Róża strains to listen above the rush of blood in her ears. She hears a German say, "I will tour your sheds and barns."

Róża inhales, bracing herself, one hand on Shira's wrist. A clump of moist dirt slides down her neck and into her shirt, settling at the small of her back. Minutes pass. Henryk must have taken him to the far sheds first, allowing them the time they needed to move to the dugout.

When the barn door scrapes the earthen floor and boots pound to the left of their heads, Henryk's voice comes loudly—perhaps too loudly—but steady.

"It's a basic barn as you can see."

"You have a lot of space here, the outbuildings, the barn. Yes?"

"I tend several large fields. It takes a lot of equipment."

"You could keep a second family here. Or hide a swarm of Jews—"

Róża feels as if her bowels might give way. Henryk doesn't miss a beat.

"Oh, maybe just a pretty girl to have my way with in the night. Of course, I'd have to kill the rest of her family—"

The soldier laughs. His tone is friendlier now.

The conversation is muffled for a moment. Then Róża hears:

"We need your barn for storing supplies. I'll give you four days to clear it out."

So this is it.

"Of course," Henryk says, sounding lighthearted. "I will clean out some space and, you know, get my girl out before the wife sees."

The clomp of boots recedes. The barn door scrapes shut. For several moments, Róża holds herself frozen. What will become of them?

She waits a long while before moving Shira back to the loft. Once there she insists they remain buried beneath the hay. She weighs their options: The Gracja ghetto? The woods? The merchant's house?

At nightfall, Krystyna steps inside with food.

"Róża."

Róża attempts to disentangle herself from the hay, to stand, but her legs shake terribly. "I know."

Krystyna's pails hold twice as much as usual—barley soup *and* radish salad. She speaks in the most formal Polish, coded to keep the conversation above Shira's comprehension. Arrangements for Shira are nearly set: false papers, a transport plan, her placement in a convent orphanage.

"Where?" Róża asks.

"In Celestyn."

"How far is that from here?"

"Others refused, Róża. This one said yes."

"But how far?"

"Nearly three hundred kilometers, due south."

Three hundred kilometers! Róża slides back to sitting and gathers Shira close.

What better alternative does she have?

She can't know what safety she can secure for Shira, with her *or* apart. She tightens her clasp around her girl, her lips moving in a loop of prayer. With every sound from outside the barn—the ricochet of voices, the creak of wagon wheels, the slow clop of horses' hooves—she seizes up with fear.

The streets are quiet now—the Germans have gone from the village, no ruckus even from the tavern—yet her mother won't let Shira out of her grasp. Shira shifts to evade her mother's scent, breath like turned milk, and peers through a wall crack. Her mother strokes Shira's cheek, over and over, presses her face to her neck. When Shira asks what's wrong, her mother looks away, mumbling.

The following day, Shira notices Krystyna with a lady she doesn't remember seeing before. Arms hooked and heads bent together, they walk a full circle around the barn. Later, Krystyna stands on the loft ladder and whispers to her mother in big, winding words. Her mother nods knowingly but searches Krystyna's face the way a lost person searches a map. Again, the pail has more food than they're used to, so Shira eats and eats, happy to stuff herself. A full belly hurts her mother, but not her.

When Henryk comes in, Shira isn't made to hide. In fact, he has clothes for her tucked inside his jacket: a dress made of yellow gingham, only slightly frayed at the collar, and larger shoes. She trades out the shoes immediately, stretching her crushed pinkie toes. She is to try the dress on tomorrow when she wakes.

At bedtime, her mother doesn't seem at all tired, so Shira tries to stay awake, but her belly is full and her eyelids heavy, and with the funny thought of her yellow bird hopping across the lines of a new musical composition, chirping out its melody, Shira falls asleep.

Krystyna comes into the barn at dawn. "Is Shira awake?"

"Not yet," Róża whispers. "Last night's meal has kept her sleeping soundly."

"Good. My sister was here yesterday. Everything is set. She will come for her late tonight. We can't risk waiting."

Róża cannot speak for the tight lump in her throat.

"This is for you." Krystyna holds a card with an address printed on it. "When the war is over—when it is safe—you will go and get Shira."

Róża grasps the card, which reads, "Siostry Felicjanki, ul. Poniatowskiego 33, Celestyn"; yet she holds it away at arm's distance. She's not sure she can go through with this.

"Róża, it is her best chance."

She looks away.

"What is the plan for *you*?" Krystyna asks.

"My cousin Leyb fled to the woods. I will try to find him." Since news of the burned-down barn in the adjacent village, Róża has given up on her plan to try with the merchant's wife. And returning to Gracja isn't an option, as Henryk just heard the Gracja ghetto has been sealed and subjected to several *Aktionen*.

"Are you sure the woods—"

"I don't have anywhere else to go."

Chapter 21

Róża tugs the shred of blanket, once pink but now a hay-coated dull gray, from Shira's sleeping grasp and settles herself, needle and thread in hand, in the shaft of light that beams in through the largest crack in the loft wall. There she stitches letter after tiny letter, spelling out Shira's name in the blanket's ragged, already bumpy seam.

With each yank of thread, Róża's thoughts dart between her mother and her little girl, between unspeakable sorrow and fear. Her mother is the one who taught Róża to sew. Late afternoons nestled on the plush sitting room sofa, she guided Róża's small hand with her own thick one, patiently and encouragingly, the faint scent of celeriac upon her breath. Róża remembers bow-tie cookies baking in the kitchen, the rhythmic whoosh-whooshing of a wood plane emanating from her father's workshop, an orchestra's recording the constant background.

When would Róża ever sit with Shira like that, in comfort, with abundant food and music, teaching her daughter the things she knows?

Róża pauses in her sewing to reach for the one thing she

has of her mother's: the metal frosting tip, small enough to fit on Róża's finger like a thimble. She's kept it in her own pocket since that day in the closet.

Always, her mother tucked raspberry jam or fresh cherries into the center of her cakes, and drew grand, elegant designs with her frosting. As a child, Róża would stare up at the finished cakes in wonder.

"They're beautiful, Mama."

Her mother beamed. "There is a saying I believe in, that 'beauty will save the world.'"

Why hadn't Róża shared this with Shira? She vows that she will when Shira wakes.

From within the farmhouse, Łukasz squeals. Along the lane, hooves echo in the distance. In the loft, Shira sleeps on, one hand sticking out from the hay, loosely cupped. Róża's choked breath comes out as a shudder.

Róża wipes her stinging eyes and coaxes the needle into position with continued, painstaking care. She must be precise, tucking the stitches *beneath* the piping so that they don't protrude in any way, so that they are hidden. When she finishes, the name sewn into the blanket's edge is invisible. Nearly.

Henryk comes in next with what looks like a bucket of earth. He pulls out a variety of leaves and roots and explains which are edible, which poisonous.

"Some different things will grow in the deep woods, but you can follow basic rules: Avoid plants that have finely toothed, narrow-pointed leaves like these. You mustn't eat white berries. The mushrooms that have a slightly green cap are the most dangerous—be careful. Also, do you know anything about tracks?"

"No, I—"

"Others' tracks and your own—you'll need to watch for them. Don't strike the ground with your heel. Step and pull back, so it seems you are traveling in the opposite direction. If your prints are very noticeable, wear socks over your boots. I brought you a few warm things."

He kisses her tenderly, stopping only when Shira wakes and turns their way.

Shira stares at patterns in the hay, and soon she's imagining: weaving a basket for a hot-air balloon, constructing a hay ladder to the moon, laying down a roadway out of the barn. If she were to set the stalks down end to end, would they take her as far as the meadow? Would they take her all the way home? She extends a single strand toward the silvery spiderweb slung in the low corner between a rafter and the loft wall. She doesn't poke at its intricate threads, doesn't cause the small black spider to scurry and build a new home.

Her mother's whisperings—"Shall I tell you more of *The Snow Maiden*, I don't think I explained the whole story; or would you rather I read to you a bit?"—have a false ring, so Shira overrides them with a noise: a squeaky single-note chirp, louder than she intended.

As soon as the chirp leaves Shira's mouth, she regrets it. Her mother rears at her, pale and puffy faced. Worse than a harsh scolding is the dented look in her eyes.

Shira retreats, contrite. Hardly moving, she changes into the new dress Henryk brought her. She wants to stand up and twirl, see how the skirt swings in the air, but she stays down, still and silent, clutching her blanket. There are new bumps at the blanket's seam. Shira doesn't ask her mother about them. She'll ask later, when her mother is happy again.

Henryk comes into the barn in broad daylight. He perches on the loft ladder and speaks to Róża in low tones, his words muffled by his bearded lips.

After he leaves Shira asks, "Does Pan Wiśniewski want to marry you?" He looks at her mother the way *Tata* did.

"What? Hush yourself!"

Shira decides to move her treasures to new hiding spots. She takes the pottery shards from the nook made by the crosstie and rafter and stows them inside a little pouch that her mother sewed her when they first arrived here and that Shira decorated with puffs of rabbit fur. The two ceramic bits she'd hidden together along the back wall of the loft she separates, hiding one on top of the crossbeam and the other behind the highest rung of the ladder, beneath hay. She opens the atlas to Africa—she is excited by the notion of an Ivory Coast—and stows some of her treasures in a corner she imagines deep inside the caves near Mount Nimba, some at the water's edge.

Her mother has bad poops in the basin. Shira pushes her face deeper in the atlas to escape the smell. She traces a finger along the arced coastline, imagining herself an explorer.

That evening, Shira waits for darkness, for her mother to tell their nightly story about the little girl in the silent flower garden. But her mother tells a different story: a story of how the little girl goes to a new garden where she can make noise, can laugh and shout, can fill up the space with her whole self rather than live scrunched like a flower in a too-small pot.

Shira scooches out of her mother's grasp. Amid the fake bright notes in her mother's voice she hears an underlying chord: heartbreak.

She stares hard at her mother, whose forced smile does not match her anguished eyes. Something is wrong. Shira wishes for the little girl in the story to compose perfect harmonies that the bird will sing—

"I need you to go to a safer place, Shira; just for a while," her mother says.

"No! Please! I won't make noise, not ever again. I'm sorry, *Mamusia*."

Her mother reaches for her hand but squeezes it too tight. Shira swallows back tears and pulls her hand away, covering herself over with hay.

Why did I ever have to chirp like that? Shira promises herself to be silent and still, to do what her mother wants of her: to disappear.

She lies unmoving, like a stone. Music storms inside her in movements dark and gloomy, but she shows no outward signs: no tapping fingers, no bobbing feet. She doesn't scratch her itches. She holds back every sneeze. She doesn't even whisper to her little bird, who is viciously pecking at his left foot, trying to make himself like the other, outside birds.

Eventually she pleads, using her quietest voice, "Tell *our* story, Mama. Does the bird bring seeds from the poppy fields?"

Her mama's face looks sunken and tired; new lines etch her forehead. She seems not to have heard Shira's question. When she finally speaks, she tells the story of how, with the daisies from their garden, the little girl and her mother weave a magical flower chain that can expand to any length, connecting them.

"However far apart they wander, they can always feel each other if they tug on the chain."

"But they are always together!"

Tears spring to Shira's eyes. She continues the protest in her mind: *The mama and her little girl could never* really *be connected by a chain of daisies! It would break apart; it would tangle and they would trip. She should know this— the mama and her girl have to stay together!* But Shira does not dare protest aloud. Not when quiet might fix things.

Her mother doesn't continue with the story, and Shira doesn't ask her to. Silently, Shira shapes bits of hay into new nests. Her bird hops past these and nestles low in the cup of her hands.

Eventually Shira settles into the hay to sleep, but her mother is fidgety. Her breath sounds heavy and ragged.

"Mama?"

"I've had to make a different plan for you."

"No, Mama, please! Give me another chance! I didn't mean to be loud before."

"You've done nothing wrong, Shira. It is just that there is a better place."

"But—"

"We can't stay here any longer. And this new place is going to be good for you. You'll be with other children, you'll have space to run and play."

A single moment in which Shira *wants* to go to the better place, even apart from her mother, until her fear overrides it—

"Please, Mama. Not without you!"

Shira clings to her mother, digs her fingers into her flesh as Róża lifts Shira out of the hay and carries her down the ladder. It creaks noisily, yet despite the noise, her mother does not stop until she reaches the ground with Shira still hanging on, frantic.

Will there be giants?

An unfamiliar woman steps through the barn door, bringing gusts of cold air with her. Shira can't make out her features, bundled as she is against winter, just her pale blue eyes that sweep the barn and come to rest on Shira.

"Mama, no!"

"Only for a little while, my darling—"

Shira begins to cry. Her mother kneels down so that they are level. Shira raises her palms, waiting for her mother to fold her large fingers around them, but instead her mother thrusts her blanket into her hands.

"Be sure to keep this with you. I've stitched the letters of your name—"

Shira buries herself in her mother, eyes squeezed tight, fingers clenched around her.

Kisses wet her cheeks. Shira opens her eyes. Her mother is still kneeling there, unwrapping Shira's fingers from her arms.

Shira breathes in her mother's sharp, grassy scent. She looks at the ladder leading to the barn loft.

"Mama?"

"I love you with all my heart," her mother says, her face going liquid like melted snow sliding from an eave.

Everything happens so quickly after that. The lady whisks Shira out of the barn and down the lane past rows of sleeping houses. The air is frigid. It burns Shira's eyes as, panicked, she struggles to look around her. *Where is she taking me?*

The darkness outside is different from the dark of the barn—the moonlight reflects brightly off the snow, causing a blinding glow—and Shira has to blink several times to see anything at all.

"Come, sweet," the lady coaxes. Her voice is gentle, but

her grip is tight. She leads Shira off the lane to a footpath, thick with snow. Shira twists to look back, to see the barn, but the lady tugs her forward and along, uphill, then down. Shira can hardly catch her breath. A sharp, cramping pain seizes her side and she feels overcome with nausea. She hasn't taken more than a few steps in months, and this air is freezing her tongue and tearing at her lungs. She wants to stop. She wants to scream and kick, to make a commotion, but her training in silence stifles her. Snow saturates her shoes, and her toes ache with cold as she is dragged on and on. Tears that well up freeze, icy, on her eyelashes.

"It's not far now—just down this pathway."

As she is led farther away from the barn, Shira searches the tree branches for birds, for *her* bird, but she sees only dark shadows. Her mother's words—"I need you to go to a safer place"—ring in her head. There *is* no safe place without her mother! Shira feels her feet slipping beneath her as the lady tugs on and talks her out of the only life she knows:

"You are to call yourself Zosia—a good Catholic name— from now on. Do you understand? You are not to be Shira, not to anyone."

Shira bites at her salty lips. *No,* she protests in her head, *my name is not Zosia!*

Shira knows that she is supposed to hide, but she wants to be Shira still, and she wants to be with her mother! She lifts her blanket to the moonlight, searching for the letters her mother stitched.

"I need you to listen to what I'm telling you. From now on, your parents are named Agnieszka and Bolesław. You have never before set foot in Gracja. That you have hidden in Bielsk, in a farmer's barn—you must forget every detail of it. Zosia?"

The lady's eyes are like big blue marbles; worry lives in the lines around her mouth.

Shira feels a stabbing in her heart. She has only ever known her parents as Mama and *Tata*. Why is this lady calling them strange names? She tries to wrench her hand away—she wants to run back to the barn, she wants to be with her mother—but the lady's clasp on her is too tight.

The path narrows and the woods thicken. Protruding tree roots batter Shira's toes and trip up her feet. Shira sputters out words: "Where . . . are you . . . taking me? I want . . . to go back!" All she can see are trees until she spots a house, a carriage parked beside it, tucked at the bottom of a wooded hill.

"Here now," the lady says. "Come in the house."

In the front hallway, the lady is tucking papers into different pockets of her coat, all the while muttering how Zosia cannot possibly pass, not with her hair; they'll need cover, darkness above all, as she has no bleach here. Shira doesn't know what she's talking about; she is awed by the brightness and warmth of the house. Unlike what she could see of Krystyna and Henryk's, there are pretty paintings on the walls, books scattered in piles, and, most incredibly, a small stack of sheet music. Shira stares at it, her breath still heaving.

"You like music?"

Shira gives a single scared nod.

It had been through the stir of *notes*—from her mother's cello, her father's violin—that Shira could know her parents' truest feelings. And her dear grandfather's, from the symphonies he listened to, hunched at his workbench amid chisels and planers, wood pieces and string.

The lady leads Shira into the kitchen. On the table sits a

plate of cookies. Shira eats one cookie and puts another in her pocket for her mother. The lady is explaining that *her* name is Maryla and that she must teach Shira the Lord's Prayer, what people call the "Our Father," right away.

Shira does not dare repeat the words. She makes no sound at all. But as her eyes adjust to the lantern light, Shira recognizes Maryla—she's the one who circled the barn, arm in arm with Krystyna. Shira feels a wave of relief: Maryla will take Shira back to the barn, back to her mother. Or she will bring her mother here!

There is a bath basin by the stove into which Maryla pours hot kettle water into cold. "This should warm things up. Quick, hop in." Shira allows Maryla to pull off her dress and shoes and place her into the basin. The soothing warmth causes her to shiver. She wriggles her battered toes, sore despite the larger-sized shoes Henryk gave her. She dunks her head and splashes about like an eel. She stills, letting Maryla delouse her and scrub her clean. Music plays in her head, jaunty, like a dance; perhaps she will try to write it out later on her music paper.

Afterward, when dried and bundled up, she lets Maryla walk her outside. Shira seeks out the direction of the barn and tugs Maryla with all her strength.

"We have to go get my mother!"

"No, Zosia." Maryla drags Shira to the carriage. Pressed close, Shira's nostrils fill with Maryla's unfamiliar, citrusy scent. She tries once again to wriggle out of Maryla's grasp.

"I need you to get in this minute. We have to move while it's still dark." Maryla hands Shira her blanket.

The back of the carriage is strewn with yellow straw. Maryla hoists Shira in. She opens a flask and brings it to

Shira's lips. "Now please, take a drink. It's chocolaty, and it will help you sleep."

Shira takes a swig of the thick, syrupy liquid, sweet on her tongue and warm in the low of her belly. Maryla presses Shira's shoulders until she is lying entirely flat and covers her over. "No sitting up," she says, before climbing up front.

As the carriage lurches forward, Shira is jostled hard against the floor. The thick straw muffles her cries.

Shira turns her head every which way without moving her body. All she can see through the straw are the black-painted sides of the carriage. *Why did I wish, even for a moment, to leave the barn?* She cries anew, thinking of the contorted expression on her mother's face as she bade her to go.

Her eyes sting and burn, and she squeezes them shut as the carriage ride grows steady and rhythmic. Helpless, she tries to do what she's seen her mother do: mouth silent prayers, over and over. *Please. God.* But she feels herself growing thick tongued and logy. Despite her terror, the repetitious movement of the carriage lulls her. She wants it all to be a dream; she wants to fall asleep and wake lying beneath the hay beside her mother.

Instead, she will wake in a cast-iron bed amid several rows of beds. And the life she's known—tales of an enchanted garden, the whisper-hum of a lullaby as she falls asleep, the soft folding of her mother's hand over hers—will be replaced by a cold hush, barren white walls, a single dark carving of a man, arms stretched, head hung in sorrow. She will no longer be Shira. The name chalked on a slate by her bedside will be "Zosia."

Chapter 22

Krystyna and Henryk step into the barn. Krystyna holds a wrapped-up food package; Henryk, his own thickest pair of socks. Róża is anguished, crying. Krystyna pulls her close. "I will be praying for you both." She smells faintly of onions.

Róża straightens up, nodding her gratitude, looking from Krystyna to Henryk through her tears. Henryk's eyes meet hers quickly, before he bows his head and looks away. "Goodbye," he says formally.

They press their goods on her and walk out.

Róża pulls Natan's fur hat over her ears and steps into the muck boots that stand like sentries at the corner of the barn. She layers a spare barn coat over her own woolen one and stuffs its oversize pockets with the few possessions she has: the card fold of photographs, her mother's frosting tip, Natan's compass and broken watch, a mess of yarn and thread. The card with the address of Siostry Felicjanki printed on it, she hides temporarily inside the booted cuff of her pant leg. She hates to take more, but she grabs a canteen and matches,

Henryk's root clippers, a trowel, and two blunt knives that she stuffs into the spare socks so they won't chink. Finally, she reaches for a small pot she can use to make a fire in. She places Krystyna's food package inside and loops its handle over her arm.

Gripping the compass, she pushes open the barn door. A gust of freezing wind tears at her skin. Along the lane, thin scarves of smoke drift from the chimneys of dark houses. Róża blinks at the snow's moonlit reflection, wary of her eyes. Is someone afoot or standing by a window, looking out? There's been a swirl of action here tonight. She raises the collars of her double coats to shield her face. Like everything from the barn, the coats smell of damp hay and Henryk. She walks briskly, then breaks into a run, away from the village, in the direction of the woods.

With every step, Róża fights the sting in her thighs, the roiling bile in her stomach, the biting cold at her nose and cheeks and fingertips. She pushes on despite the pain and atrophy, despite her acute desire to stop and rest. She tries to outrun her loss.

When Maryla had stepped into the barn, all Róża wanted was to call off the plan, to send Maryla away and find a different hiding place for her and Shira, together. But it was no good, the two of them on the run in freezing temperatures with no promise of shelter. She had to get Shira to safety. So she'd struggled to keep steady, to meet Shira's gaze, but then Shira put out her hands—for Róża to fold her large fingers over Shira's small ones, their good-night ritual—and when that didn't work, Shira grasped Róża's arms, dug in her nails.

"Oh, Shira—"

The imprint of Shira's fingers still pressed upon her arms; the shrill tone of Shira's voice rang on in her ears. Shira had clung to her and Róża had pried her off. Finger by tiny finger. Róża felt flayed, a layer of her own self ripped and taken—

Róża's legs give out at the northern edge of the woods, where, still, she knows she could be spotted. She needs a place to hide.

At the forest's perimeter, Róża finds a large fallen tree limb, its branches thick with pine needles. If she can build up its sides, it can serve, just temporarily until she can find something better. She gulps water, unpacks Krystyna's package, and takes two greedy bites of onion bread, then sets to work creating a burrow packed tight with pine needles. She pulls branches over it in all but one corner that she keeps open for the firepot. Finally she climbs in, breathing heavily, staring up through the branches at the blue-black sky.

Sometime in the night she wakes. Icy bits of leaf and bark have blown in through the gaps of pine branches and pebbled between her teeth. She grinds and swallows. The ground is hard beneath her shoulders and buttocks, and every part of her aches with stiffness and cold. Except her toes: Róża cannot feel them at all. She transfers the address card to her pocket and heaves off her boots, pulling on Henryk's socks, tucking her numbed feet, one at a time, into the crook of her bent knees.

She wakes again because of a sound—an animal call. She shifts her weight, sweeps the top branches away, and sits upright. She wonders what might be near: bats, boars, a wolf? She listens intently to hear beyond the gusting wind. A bird?

She lies back down in her shelter and tries again to sleep,

but her mind floods with memories of Shira. The timbre of her voice. The oily smell of her hair, the warm dough of her cheek. The weight of her arms, her legs, draped in sleep.

Despite her longing, there is a flash of relief—she doesn't have to feed Shira or warm her or concoct tales of magical flowers or musical birds—before a punishing guilt, as her head swirls with all that might have gone wrong with Shira's transport to the nuns. She hauls the mass of branches over her like a door closing shut. Inside her burrow, she curls herself in a tight ball and averts her eyes from the accusing stars.

Part 2

The little girl does not dare cry out. If there are giants in this new garden, she doesn't want them to hear her. The yellow bird sings her music, and the enchanted flowers grow. Still, the girl remains silent. Her mother told her that an invisible daisy chain would connect them always, and she tries to feel its gentle tug. But deep down the girl knows: Until she is with her mother, wrapped in her arms, she will remain lost.

Chapter 23

The morning light is just breaking when a young nun in long brown robes stands over Zosia and makes the sign of the cross above her forehead. Zosia jerks awake with a start, staring first at the nun—her starched headdress like horns—then at the rows of beds, white sheets pulled pin tight. Frantic, Zosia kicks against the bedcovers that trap her, stiff and coarse and smelling of lye. With one hand, she clutches her tattered blanket, and with the other, she cups her fingers into a nest.

A single small window, pitched too high for Zosia to see out of, is trimmed with dark wood, stark against the unadorned white walls. The room's chill air feels sharp in Zosia's chest, without the warmth of her mother. Whether from cold or fear, Zosia begins to tremble. The nun gently presses her hand on Zosia's chest like a weight on a fluttering slip of paper, a steadying force, and after several flaps, a shudder, a flinch, Zosia's body gradually acquiesces.

"There, there. Don't be scared. My name is Sister Alicja." Sister Alicja looks from the slate to the girl. "And you must be Zosia."

Zosia involuntarily blinks as if to will away the name—not her own, not given by her mother. She pulls her blanket closer.

"Zosia, yes," Sister Alicja repeats, as if the name is merely something to agree upon. Her round face is shiny and clean. After a few moments, she holds up a small brown dress and a white sleeveless smock. "Come, put these on."

As Zosia stands, she shoves her hand into her pocket, clinging to the crumbled bits of cookie she'd taken for her mother. She doesn't want to change dresses, no matter how filthy hers is, but Sister Alicja tugs her out of the old and into the new, quickly, eyes averted all the while.

"Here's a roll to eat. While the other children are in the refectory, we'll do something about that hair of yours."

Zosia puts a hand to her hair. Maryla didn't rebraid it after her bath and now it is tangled.

Sister Alicja guides her to a nearby bathroom. A single bulb casts a dim yellow circle on two toilet stalls and a large trough sink. Stiff washcloths and towels in neatly folded squares line the rough shelving above. Sister Alicja reaches for a towel.

Zosia struggles as the back of her head is pressed against the sink's cold porcelain rim and a liquid—so sharp odored and pungent that Zosia's nostrils burn just to breathe it—is poured into her hair. She wriggles and rears up, but Sister Alicja presses her back down, gently but firmly. "Now, now." Wrapping a towel around Zosia's shoulders, she guides her to a sitting position and produces a second roll for her to eat. "We'll need to wait a bit for it to work."

Sister Alicja runs freezing water to the very edge of Zosia's hairline and the base of her neck. Zosia stares up at a crack in the white ceiling plaster to keep from screaming;

she shivers as the water soaks her collar and trickles down her back.

"We don't have hot water for this. I'm sorry."

After a few more rinses, Sister Alicja dries Zosia's hair with a towel. Zosia's nose burns, and the back of her dress is damp. Her eyes fix on Sister Alicja's headdress, the tuck of her skin beneath the white rising rim, the fall of black veil. It looks to Zosia as if Sister Alicja has no hair at all.

With a few final pats, Sister Alicja removes the towel from Zosia's head.

"That's plenty light."

Zosia grabs a clump and pulls it forward so she can look at it. She'd thought the washing was to get her hair cleaner, but now she sees it was to change its color: it is near white. She gasps, shocked.

Sister Alicja puts her steady hands on Zosia's shoulders and speaks kindly.

"It's just hair. It will be better this way. But wait . . ." She presses Zosia back into a sitting position with her head tilted back and dabs at Zosia's eyebrows with a bleach-soaked towel. "I need you to keep still a bit longer, eyes closed. It's no use if your eyebrows are dark, is it?"

A few minutes later, the nun takes another appraising look, her smile pursed. With a quick nod, she wipes any residue of bleach from Zosia's eyebrows, then rotates Zosia and, section by section, brushes through her knotty, now-strawlike hair and dries it again with a towel.

Zosia's eyes sting with tears. She does not understand why Sister Alicja is doing this. But before she can ask, Sister Alicja guides Zosia down a dark corridor, past thick columns and vaulted archways, strange and intimidating. Zosia startles as, with each footfall, Sister Alicja's stiff-heeled shoes sound loudly upon the wood floor. She looks for windows, a door—a way to escape—but finds herself stopped by the shock of noise everywhere around her. Footsteps and singing. Bells marking off the hour. So much sound after so much silence.

Outside in the courtyard, Zosia hears the shrieks of boys, one tagging another, then running off; the singsong patter of girls, counting as they jump; the sharp-edged admonishments of nuns, instructing and cajoling. She thinks back to Henryk's boys at play—the sounds that brought no danger. She remembers her own chirp reverberating in the barn—the sound that had cost her everything.

Zosia stands motionless, still fighting back tears, her eyes searching for hiding places in the stone walls, behind the hedges. The children are lanky and fair. Not one has thick dark hair like her mother has. Like she had.

As soon as they spot her, the children swarm her at once and stare. Zosia shifts soundlessly from foot to foot, unaccustomed to being looked at. A lone girl greets her with "Hallo," but Zosia's voice chokes. Words, to Zosia, are like glass beads around her neck. If one were to break loose, they would all clatter to the floor and scatter, shatter the quiet that kept her and her mother alive, entwined beneath hay.

At lunch, when Zosia brings the spoon to her mouth, her lips don't open with a smack, her teeth don't click as she chews, her throat makes no gulping sounds as she swallows. Her hips never once shift upon the hard refectory bench, her starched sleeves don't rustle against the napkin in her lap. She is meant to hide here in plain sight; this much she knows, even if she does not know why. There is a din in the room: the chatter and slurping of the other children, the quick slap-slap of the nuns' soles upon the floor, and the solemn utterance of prayer. Zosia makes no sound at all and keeps her eyes on her food. It is more than she is used to. Soup, tinged orange with carrots, and a mound of potatoes on the side.

She eats greedily at first but slows, thinking of her mother: all the times she didn't eat while, outside with Krystyna, Zosia gobbled bread and butter and eggs.

In the afternoon, Sister Alicja ushers Zosia past murky portraits of people with golden halos. "This is Saint Francis of Assisi, and that is Saint Elizabeth of Hungary," and on into the chapel. Every other part of the convent is bare and dingy, reeking of bleach, the same as her hair. But the chapel is wondrous, arched and gleaming. Sunlight floods through high windows, and candles flicker on a table at the front, giving off a waxy scent. All around is a radiating calm.

Alicja guides Zosia into a row behind several other children and gestures for her to copy them as they set down the cushions for kneeling and reach for the hymnals lining the bench backs. Zosia sinks into the hushed stillness, the quiet here expectant, not at all like the oppressed silence of the barn. She feels shaky, confused. Once on her knees in her row, she drops beneath the pew entirely, curls tight, and cries silently.

She tries to soothe herself by filling her head with her mother's voice—the only sound that comforted her in danger. The particular lilt and catch when she whisper-sang about the hen who brought glasses of tea to her chicks. *Cucuricoo! Di mom iz nisht do* . . . Her mother would speak to her in many languages. Polish. Russian. German. Ukrainian. But always, she sang in Yiddish, in notes lyrical and haunting.

A loud burst of real singing interrupts Zosia's reverie. She twists around to see a group of nuns standing in two lines at the back of the church. Zosia doesn't know the language of the song, but her heart delights at the joyous interweaving of voices, some deep and resonant, others high and bell-like. She stops crying and sits up. The sound is miraculous, like the broke-open sky—the sky they sat under, she and her mother, in the hills and the pastures, before all the walking stopped. Before the rafters and roofs trapped them in. Before her mother sent her away.

Chapter 24

Winter 1943

Róża heads for the deepest forest, praying that the bitter cold will keep patrolling soldiers nearer to the perimeter. As a distraction from her hunger, she invents a story to remember the convent location, a story about a brave prince named Józef, who at thirty-three crosses a long bridge while looking up at the heavens. She thinks how Shira would like this story—with the clues for ul. Poniatowskiego 33, Celestyn, contained within it—and how she would have questions about the ways Józef was brave, and what the heavens looked like, and what his family did to celebrate his thirty-third birthday. The actual address card, too dangerous to be loose, she has sewn invisibly into the waistband of her pants. She trains her eyes on the crystallized tree branches, a glittering wonderland despite a world gone wrong.

In this vast primeval wood, trees lean in every direction. Bare trunks rise out of the thick undergrowth; others lie crosswise on the floor, lined with snow. Fallen boughs are everywhere. Róża skirts patches of bramble as she hauls loose branches to the mouth of a recessed rock cave. She burrows inside and attempts to fashion a bow using a thin but sturdy stick and long threads from Henryk's jacket. At first, the contraption reminds her of a violin bow, Natan's, until she cuts the tip sharp enough to kill a small animal.

She attends to the sounds of the woods. It is far from silent here, her own presence marked by the shrieks of birds and the warning *kuks* of squirrels. She notices patterns in the wind; for a long time she tracks the movement of a grouse.

She worries that fire—which she needs desperately for keeping warm—will expose her in hiding, whether by flame or by smoke. At first, she builds a small blaze inside her pot, tindering it with the driest layers of tree bark so as to minimize the smoke. But the idea of making soup in the pot, even if just hot water and some roots, anything to heat her insides, drives her to attempt a small ground fire. In a thicketed area she mounds dead pine branches, dumps the burning embers from the pot on top, and prays the open blaze will go unnoticed. She cleans the pot, adds water and two handfuls of birch root, and sets it upon the fire.

When she walks about, she rolls her feet so as to leave the scantest trace. She forages the forest floor for acorns, mushrooms, and wild garlic, rare to find, beneath the snow, and breaks through the ice blanketing the swamplands to fill her canteen. Weak with hunger, she remains hidden during daylight and moves only at nightfall, after dark.

Róża uses twine to refasten the curling-away soles of Henryk's boots. Without them, she knows, she will die here in the woods. She darns the holes in her mittens and pulls Natan's fur hat over her wind-bitten ears, looking skyward to assess the moon. Before setting out, she ties a knot into a length of thread to mark her survival of another day.

Near dawn on her third day in the woods, she eats a meal

of boiled birch bark. With no one to save for and scrimp, she devours every last stringy bite. When she burrows down again for another day's rest, Róża rubs herself warm in a refusal to give in, curl up, and die. She listens for the pulse of music within her: a melody, big and spacious, to carry her outside of her solitary anguish. In the way that other people share the stars—looking up at the exact moment, they see the same night sky—she and Shira have *this*: The soar of violins mixing with cellos. The flight of notes, like wingbeats, that transport them together, beyond the confines of a forest burrow, a convent wall.

The convent is a winding maze of corridors that Zosia does not yet understand, so she follows the other girls, shivery in their thin starched dresses, as they shuttle from class to chore to chapel. They slow their steps only as they pass by the woodstoves, where they huddle briefly to warm themselves before rushing on. In the children's quarters, there are just two stoves, one in the community room and one in the corridor outside their bedchamber.

Ula and Adela act bossy, as if they are the nuns and the other girls are their wards. A pale, reedy girl, Kasia—the same girl who said "hallo" to Zosia her first day and, really, the only one who talks to Zosia—complains. "Why do I have to wash again, just because Ula says so? My hands are clean." Zosia doesn't dare say anything. She's noticed Ula staring at her hair and Adela crinkling her nose and fixing her eyes on Zosia's worn-out shoes.

She tails the group as they move through the corridors, past the paintings of sad-faced saints. She peers into different rooms along the way.

In the afternoon of her fifth day in the convent, the sight of a small violin stops Zosia in her tracks. She stands, solitary, before an open doorway, breathless.

The violin, amber, with thin black streaks along its belly, rests on a desk in a classroom strewn with other instruments: an accordion, two guitars, assorted drums and triangles. Everything looks dusty and unused. *Did they once hold music lessons here? Do they still?*

From the threshold, Zosia stares at the violin in wonder. Her grandfather's workshop was full of these—honey timbred and smelling of spruce and resin and glue and varnish—and there was the one with the star that her father played, head cocked and arm flying in the evening, whose strings he let *her* press as he moved the long bow up and down.

A few beats, and Zosia tears herself away to rejoin the others. But she memorizes her way back, and over the course of several days she inches her way through the doorway and into the room until, finally, she stands before the violin, her fingers aching to touch the taut strings and the smooth curve of its scroll. Kasia—two years a ward, orphaned, and then separated from her only sister—follows Zosia and asks her why she wants to keep visiting the violin. Zosia only shrugs. Whether she remembers or just imagines it, the violin conjures her mother holding her high in the air, dancing round and round to Gypsy rhythms, quick and exciting.

The next day during yard time, a nun called Sister Nadzieja asks Zosia to follow her inside to the classroom. Zosia fears she is in trouble, but Sister Nadzieja smiles kindly. Except for the violin, all of the instruments have been put away, and the violin looks clean, even shiny.

"I passed by here yesterday as you were admiring the violin. Would you like to try and play it?"

A bow now rests beside the violin, and Zosia sees that both are sized for a child. By way of demonstration, Sister Nadzieja lifts the violin to her chin and with a scrunched arm moves the bow steadily across the strings. The sound is round and smooth and *loud*. Zosia takes a step back, scared.

"When you play, the way you stand is very important. Also the way you hold the bow." Sister Nadzieja's words rise up as if from an underground cavern, deep and comforting, and her eyes remind Zosia of the chestnuts she and her mother found, fallen from a tree in the pasture.

Sister Nadzieja kneels down and arranges Zosia's feet to be at shoulder's width beneath her. She shapes her hand around the bow, her littlest finger curled up upon the screw, her first finger upon the pad. She positions the violin, tilted to the side beneath Zosia's turned elbow, and places the rest under Zosia's chin. Finally, holding Zosia's hand, she guides the bow up and down along the D string.

With Nadzieja's steady hand upon hers, the sound reverberating close to Zosia's ear is crisp and strong. Zosia freezes midstroke, terrified of what she might be giving away. Such sound as this, rich and whole, might be for others to make, but not for her. Tears stream down her cheeks.

"That was a wonderful first try!"

Zosia had been too small to hold her father's violin by herself, though she'd often imagined it. How she longs to run the bow across the strings again and hear its reverberating note.

"Now, once more," Sister Nadzieja urges.

In Zosia's thin arms even the little violin sags; the bow founders in her hand, and the sound becomes airy and uncertain. But Nadzieja stands by, supporting her arms, encouraging her to keep at it. Sister Nadzieja is a friend of

Sister Alicja's and *she* doesn't seem to think there's danger in the sound. And what it gives Zosia—standing with planted feet, the sense that her trapped-in feelings count enough to resonate beyond—is more than she has had here. Her strokes grow longer and more even.

Zosia returns to the classroom whenever she can: before breakfast and after chores. She practices everything Sister Nadzieja teaches her. Scales and arpeggios. Simple songs. Pressing her cheek, deep angled, to the violin, she plays what she hears in her head. Sister Nadzieja praises her playing and Zosia flushes with pleasure as she continues on, reaching for the sounds she remembers floating from the parlor of her Gracja home.

In time, Zosia's notes, rounded, long, and melodious or plucked, short, and halting, come to feel safe, safer even than silence. They accumulate and order themselves in Zosia's head, as monologues, as dialogues. As arguments. As pleas. As the simplest of prayers: for her mother to appear, to take her back.

Chapter 25

When she is on the move through the woods, Róża trains her eyes on the rippled patterns that wind gusts carve into fallen snow and on the prisms of colored light that dapple the white forest floor. She propels herself forward, rubbing her thumb against the smooth wooden handle of her trowel—the single most important tool she has, the thing keeping her alive—as she digs out shelter, digs out roots. When she makes a fire, she sees flickers of indigo, rare amid the yellow-orange flames. But when she closes her eyes, Róża sees only darkness.

She sets animal traps the way Henryk told her, yet each time she checks them, weak but hopeful, they gape empty. Misery overtakes her, as she is a failure at hunting, and she knows that what vegetation lurks under snow here is not enough to subsist on. She shivers constantly. It's safer, and better for foraging, to move camps, but maintaining a fire conserves matches—and she has just twenty-two left. If she dies here, from hunger or cold, she will leave Shira utterly alone.

In a dugout framed by thin crossing boughs, Róża loses

track of time and place. She has no sense of whether she's slept, how long it's been since she's last eaten. She no longer knows how many sunsets have passed, how many knots to tie on her string.

Delirium delivers a dust storm, sand whipping at her skin, stripping the flesh from her bones. Burial by a cacophony of sound—the pounding of drums, the whirling strum of guitars, the wail of bagpipes—too loud to bear. She pounds her head against the dirt floor, hoping to make it stop.

She closes her eyes to dream-images of Shira—curled up and listening to lullabies, one hand holding her tiny imaginary bird, the other her blanket—and her dreams conjure the stitches she hid amid the blanket's piping. Róża cannot dream of Shira without her blanket, and the dreams turn into nightmares as the sewn letters—proof of her daughter's Jewishness, her name—transmute into thick vines that squeeze and strangle her child. *How could I have been so foolish?*

Róża wakes, clammy. She curls tight in her burrow, in disbelief that she is here alone, living like an animal, and that her family members, all of them, are gone from her. She cannot manage to get warm again; not now, after the sweats. The ground feels like a sheet of ice beneath her. The air is damp, and her skin could itch her into madness. If she had current news, maybe she'd learn that this horror was ending and she could get on her way, get back to Shira. But alone in the woods, she cannot know what is happening in the war.

Hastily, Róża stands up, the blustery air whipping at her scalp and hair. She chose to rest here when it was still dark, but now she sees it is an area of forest with swaths of silver birch trees, narrow and exposed. She should move deeper in, to the thick cover of oaks and pines, but she is dizzy from hunger.

Faintness drives the urge to lie down again, to sleep—but *no*. She'll die if she doesn't find more food to eat.

Not far in the distance, a yellow pin of light. There may be a farmhouse she can raid. She may find barley, potatoes, or, if she dares to imagine, turnips.

She drags herself out at dusk, her body drawn into a comma against the wind, weaving through mist-shrouded trees toward the woods' edge. Her thoughts jump about, disjointed. She wonders if Krystyna and Henryk fought once she was gone. She remembers one of her worst fights with Natan. She'd overheard him disparage her father while talking to a musician friend, referring to him as a "mechanic" rather than a craftsman of instruments—including the very one that Natan played. Natan could be haughty, disdainful of both her parents at times, yet they were always there, supporting him, doting on Shira, and allowing them time for their music. Her parents didn't have prestigious jobs like his pharmacist parents, but Róża valued the way they took part in her family's life. When she confronted Natan—perhaps he looked down on her too—he denied it, he became furious, and she became furious back. Even now she grows heated thinking about it. Whereas her agony over losing him has at times halted her in her tracks, the revival of this singular anger propels her forward, allows her to tromp past her hunger and fatigue and desperation.

She moves quickly now along a footpath, the lantern light growing brighter, until the sound of footsteps halts her. She squats low behind a large rock. A figure approaches. She can't make out features, just a fur hat and long coat.

Perhaps she is delirious again, because Róża imagines that the figure could be Henryk. Or else a suspicious neighbor—Borys, back from dragging Piotr to the village center after all this time, turning him in! As the man gets closer, Róża's breath grows jagged and uneven. The muscles in her face clench tight; her bowels roil. She is certain he'll spot her prints and come after her, but he passes her by. A young farmer she's never seen before. She hurtles back toward the center of the woods, forgetting her mission for food.

As she retreats, Róża chides herself: She must be *strong*; she can't allow herself to be defeated by her fears or her punishing imagination. She leans against a sheltering tree, forcing herself to breathe in the vanilla scent of its bark—its beauty—as methodically she sharpens her trowel blade on a rock and prepares to head deeper into the woods. She must stay alive for *Shira*, so that she can reclaim her as she promised she would, hold her close once again. With gathered resolve, she digs around several tree trunks and finds mushrooms enough to boil into a soup.

A week later, Róża spots two women huddled where she planned to dig roots. As she takes a step back, her foot lands on a branch, causing a loud crack. The women turn and stare. Róża begins to run.

"Wait! Please."

Hearing Yiddish, Róża stops.

As the women approach, Róża's heart pounds in her chest. She reaches into her pocket and clutches the sharpest object she has: root clippers. But soon she sees that their expressions mirror hers; they are filled with terror and exhaustion and desperate hope.

They look related—sisters, Róża thinks—with dark hair

and dark eyes, though one's face is soft, with rounded cheeks and wide eyes, and the other is sharper, more severe.

"We saw you foraging here yesterday," the softer-faced one says.

Róża doesn't answer. Her hand is still clenched around the clippers.

"You're alone?" This same one reaches into her coat pocket and presents an offering: a handful of just-dug roots. "Here."

"Miri!" the sharper one chides.

Róża stuffs the roots into her mouth and swallows, to stay alive even if the other will now want to kill her.

But they aren't going to kill her. They are in hiding, like her. Sisters, as Róża thought, from Warsaw before the war. The woman who gave Róża the roots—Miri—sees Róża's worn-out boots and pulls out strips of a torn work shirt for wrapping her cold feet. And even more miraculous, she shows Róża a ripped fragment of a newspaper conveying hope: news of the Red Army's advance in the siege of Leningrad. How much time since the paper's printing, she doesn't know.

Róża cannot contain her relief at being with other human beings. Women. Jews. She grills them for more recent war news. They don't have any, but the sharper sister, Chana, declares her intention to join the resistance and fight, first chance she gets.

"I'm going to make them pay for what they did to our parents, our little brother—" She bats at her red-rimmed eyes.

Miri, looking disturbed, takes Chana's hand.

"At least we can thank God that you and I are together."

"I'm sorry, I cannot thank a nonexistent being." Chana is defiant as she motions at Róża. "Maybe she has weapons?"

"Chana!"

Róża looks from one to the other. She used to be so engaged with the religious, the political. Now she hopes only to make it to Celestyn by war's end, to get Shira.

When Miri suggests that perhaps they would do better to join a family camp, such as the large extended group they met hiding farther west, Chana snorts.

"Have you forgotten, Miri? Our family is dead—our brother. Our mother."

All three go silent.

Róża doesn't talk of Shira, and it is a relief. There are the dreaming hours ahead to be haunted by her loss; to see Shira's pleading eyes, her hands outstretched.

They steer the conversation to other topics while they gather kindling. To Róża's relief, the sisters have steel and flint *and* a magnifying glass for starting fires—she needn't expend matches, at least for now. Miri tells Róża how she assisted with her father's soap-making business and how Chana, with ambitions to attend university, took part in protests against the ghetto benches segregating Jews from other students. This, before their father's business was shuttered and the university was closed. Before the *real* ghettos were formed.

Róża finds herself less weary, even a bit energized, in the sisters' company. She wants to remain with them, yet she hesitates to share a camp. But Chana tells of the corpse they came upon last week, a man with a belt noosed around his neck, pants still down from a soldier's "Jew test." Róża is shaken to think how, without a scout and in her fog of hunger, she has been unaware of others—not just Jews but Germans—in the woods. How she's been luckier than she knew.

"Might I camp with you?" Róża asks.

"Oh yes, Róża; why don't you choose your spot first?" Miri offers.

Chana makes a dramatic sweep with her arm. "Yes, wherever you'd like."

The three begin to laugh and cannot stop. Repeated arm sweeps set them off, again and again. Róża reaches a hand to touch her upturned lips, her creased eyes. She'd forgotten laughter.

Róża sleeps soundly for the first time since fleeing to the woods alone. She wakes feeling buoyed by the sisters' company, Miri's especially; still, she doesn't know whether she can stay with them. Róża's imperative is to head south toward Celestyn and wait by the border's edge until it is safe to leave the woods and claim Shira. She pulls out Natan's old compass. Seeing her, Miri looks up at the orientation of the sun.

"I need to head south," Róża says in a low voice. She walks in place as if to make headway even now. Ice in thin patches crackles, and frosted branches snap beneath her feet. Miri does not ask her why and Róża is all the more grateful to her.

"Didn't Jerzy, from the large encampment, tell us that there was a Jewish partisan group south of here?" Chana asks.

Miri looks worried. "Possibly."

"Well, we can head in that direction. There's no leaving the forest, anyway, until we can get news."

They begin the trudge southward, but Chana refuses to move camps when the temperatures are frigid. "It makes no sense, Róża! We can't make headway in this wind, and we can't keep digging out the frozen earth. Let's stay here at least until the weather grows a bit milder."

Róża concedes, but the weather does not grow milder. The winter is brutal and unending. Wood for the meager fire becomes more crucial than food.

Róża's night terrors return more vividly than ever, with images of choking threads, shattered flowerpots, yellowing matchstick bones arranged into wings. Miri reaches for Róża and rubs her back. Chana sets water to boil, throws in some scavenged roots to make a tea. Róża's story spills out between sobs—how Shira is in the convent orphanage for safekeeping; how Róża is desperate to get near there, ready to claim her at war's end. How everyone else is lost: Her mother and father. Natan.

Róża thinks back to the earliest days, pregnant with Shira, when she composed a lullaby for (her) cello and (Natan's) violin.

"Since when do you compose in six-eight time?" Natan asked, looking over the music.

"When it fits the occasion."

"Six-eight is for berceuse."

"Yes, Natan, I know."

"For lulla—" And that's when he'd rushed to take her up in his arms, hardly able to kiss her for laughing with delight. It was he who suggested the name Shira, derived from the Hebrew, meaning *song*.

Róża peers out at the ice-encased trees and shivers.

At dusk, while foraging for kindling and any possible edibles—nuts, stalks, the inner bark of pines—Róża and Miri find three pairs of horn-rimmed glasses, one sized for a small child, mangled in a heap. Róża can't manage to get warm after that, despite the fire they build. Late that night,

Chana thrusts a tiny graying capsule into Róża's hand. Cyanide.

"We both have one and we want you to have one too. In case you are trapped."

Róża blinks between Miri and Chana, sisters taking her into their fold. "Thank you," she says. She shoves the pill into her pant pocket near the sewn-in card with the convent address—her only fragment of waking hope that Shira can be found safe; that she is growing, eating, playing, still with music in her head.

Chapter 26

In the convent, food rations shrink. Mealtimes grow somber as the soup thins and the bread packs dust. By nightfall, Zosia is weak with hunger, but her bird won't settle; he hops past the cup of her hands, unable to find a comfortable nest. His wondrous eighteen-note call has changed. It is now a frantic wavering beween two notes, a tremolo, as if to erase all distance, bring her mother near to her, barely a pitch away.

Zosia's sleep comes troubled. She slips into dreams that rouse her, panicked.

Her bird is no longer yellow. His feathers are white, though the downy lower barbs are brown, and the children point and laugh. Or else he is all white and Zosia can't spot him in this place of white plaster, white curtains, starched bedsheets, and snow. When he settles to sleep beside her, she rolls onto him and squishes him—she can't protect him even from herself!

Zosia wakes with a start to find Kasia's doll on her pillow, set next to her shred of blanket. She blinks back grateful tears. In the quiet of the room—even quieter than the barn without the sound of rustling hay or rabbits or falling snow or her mother—she listens to the other girls, breathing softly in sleep. The difference between them and her, so palpable, is beyond her understanding. It is more than how they know the rituals and regimens of the convent and recite every hymn by heart; how they swarm together so easily; how she stands apart with just the little violin. More than that she has secrets buried inside, secrets she is under orders to forget and *is* forgetting, though she wishes desperately to remember.

Zosia is given a new secret when Mother Agnieszka leads her to a hiding place—a closet in the hallway of the chapel, filled with fancy white prayer robes that are quilted and stitched with shiny gold threads. At the back is a wooden partition, a false back, behind which is a smaller, interior space. Zosia peers in to see that the walls are made of rough scrap boards and the corners are studded with nails, half hammered in, half bent.

"You are to slip behind this wall and remain hidden when soldiers come. Do you understand? You are not to climb out until Sister Alicja, Sister Nadzieja, or I tell you to."

Mother Agnieszka slides the hangers back and forth along the high rod, demonstrating how a soldier might search the closet without discovering Zosia behind the partition. Zosia breathes in the starch of Mother Agnieszka's wimple and wonders if she, too, has been having trouble sleeping. Her pale, papery face looks tired.

Zosia's favorite thing about Mother Agnieszka is her singing voice: she starts off lauds each morning with clear, jewel-like notes. Also, she plays checkers with the children some nights, and she puts Ula in her place for bossing.

Still, it bothers Zosia that she is called "Mother." She is not her mother, though she is asking Zosia to hide, just as her mother did.

"I have your word that you will keep still and silent here?"

Zosia nods. She knows how to make herself invisible.

Zosia knows too—though she doesn't speak of it to Mother Agnieszka—that soldiers searched the convent the previous night. While washing up in the girls' bathroom, she heard the loud boots—giants' steps—echoing through the halls. Sister Alicja swooped in and hustled her toward the back door leading to the nuns' quarters; then, changing direction, she closed her into a toilet stall, where they waited in silence. Even after the soldiers' footsteps and shouts receded, they stayed put several minutes. Sister Alicja whispered to Zosia that ordinarily when the soldiers came, it was for what they might find in the pantry—coffee or sugar or, in earlier days, chocolate. But this time their search was wider.

The very next night, soldiers storm the convent again.

At the first sound of boots approaching, Zosia gets the nod from Sister Alicja and slips out of bed before the other children are alerted to a roll call. Zosia runs, blanket clenched in hand, down the long corridor, past the portraits of patron saints and the stone sculpture of Mary. She climbs into the chapel hall closet, pulls the door shut behind her, and crawls back behind the partition. Her nightgown snags on a nail, but she wriggles it loose and settles, rubbing her finger over the looping thread. It is cold and cramped here; it smells like sawdust and iron. But worst, it is completely dark.

When Zosia had peered into the closet earlier, light had shone in from the open door. Closed now, it is pitch-black and there doesn't seem to be enough air. Zosia opens her mouth wide, gulping. Her chest feels tight and the skin on the back of her neck prickles. She thinks of the closet in Gracja, her grandparents' thick coats at her shoulders, the barn floor dugout, her mother's hand clasped tightly to hers. Over and over, she runs her finger across the stitches in her blanket.

Zosia hears soldiers nearby. It sounds like they are overturning the chapel benches, ripping hangings from the wall. Is someone pulling open the closet door?

She hugs her knees to her chest and buries her face. She can hear that the robes are being heaved, side to side. A hanger clangs to the floor. Suddenly the sharp tip of a bayonet pierces the partition wall, inches from Zosia's left shoulder.

"Nie!" Zosia's yelp is involuntary. She leans as far back as she can and claps a hand to her mouth, praying that the tromp of boots muffled her cry. Sister Alicja's panicked voice comes from outside the door.

"You will slash the holy robes. I beg you, please, to stop that!"

"What care do I have of your robes?"

The soldiers' footsteps recede. Zosia's face wets with tears, but she doesn't dare move until, later, Sister Alicja retrieves her. Zosia begs, "Please, please let me go back to the barn with my mother. I promise, I will not make a sound—"

Alicja touches Zosia's cheek, sorrow in her eyes. After checking that the other girls have been put back to sleep, lights out, she gently leads Zosia to her bed.

Zosia sits on her hands to keep from tapping. It's a special feast day, and the church service, with a visiting priest from Holy Trinity Parish, is running extra long. For the past forty minutes Zosia's stomach has been rumbling and her eyelids have gotten nearly too heavy to hold open, so it is a surprise when the priest's Epiphany homily piques her interest.

"There may be no more popular children's game than hide-and-seek. We all know how it is played: one child closes his eyes and counts while the other children hide."

Up and down the rows of pews, listing children sit upright. Zosia pulls her hands out from under her legs and tucks them into her lap.

"With the call of 'Ready? Here I come!' the hiding children are sought out, one by one, from their hiding places. The first to be found becomes the new seeker, and the game begins anew."

Children nod at this, but the priest's face is solemn, a wrinkle at his brow.

"Do we ever stop playing it? As we get older, we spend a good part of our lives hiding from and searching for other people. We even play this game with God. Sometimes we foolishly believe we can hide from Him. Other times, it seems as if He is hiding from us."

Zosia shifts in her seat.

"Epiphany tells the story of men who journeyed in search of Christ. Even with the help of a guiding star, they had difficulty finding him. They expected he would be in Jerusalem's royal palace, yet he was in a stable in the nearby village of Bethlehem."

Jerusalem: Zosia knows this place, where Moses led the Jews after years of slavery. "Next year in Jerusalem," her grandfather would say from his pillowed seat at the head of the Passover table.

"Are we looking for Jesus in the wrong places? Worse, are we hiding our sins from His judgment?

"Jews seek to hide their crimes: the killing of Jesus; the taking of Christian blood to make matzos; the profiting from the miseries of Europe's poor. And those who aid and abet them? Just as the Jews cannot hide their sins from God, nor can those who help them. Jews are Christ haters. Those who have no limits in their love of Christ must have no limits in their battle with those who hate Him. . . ."

Zosia struggles to breathe. *She* has been hiding; is she who the priest is talking about, greedy, dirty, and evil? And are the nuns *sinning* by keeping her here? Is this why Maryla and then Mother Agnieszka vowed her to silence, why she is alone—Sisters Alicja and Nadzieja are not *really* her sisters, as she's daydreamed—and will *be* alone until her mother comes for her?

Amid the blinding winter light and the rustle of robes, Zosia feels dizzy and faint. She tries to understand whether she loves Christ, or could; whether she ever would.

Heat sears her cheeks; she is certain her face has flushed red. She looks behind her to see Ula and Adela looking at her, looking *through* her, as if they know the truth of her hiding.

When the homily is over, Zosia bursts out of the chapel. By the time others file out, she is already near the back hedge, slipping into a concealed spot between a row of plants and a stone wall. She closes her eyes, remembering a word smeared in black paint on the bakery window: *Jude*.

Sister Alicja finds her after the children have gone in for lunch.

"Zosia."

"Can I be baptized?" Zosia's voice shakes with urgency.

"What?"

"I want to be baptized."

"No, Zosia. I don't think that would be right. But you can participate in a communion ceremony with the other girls come spring."

"Will that help?"

Sister Alicja rebleaches Zosia's hair that night and arranges her chore assignment to floor bleaching the following day. As Zosia mops the dormitory landing, Ula hops up the stairs, squinting and sniffing the air.

"Where were you yesterday, Zosia? You missed the fancy Epiphany luncheon."

"And we didn't see you at bedtime the night before last." Adela has come up behind her.

"I have to finish the floor." Zosia tries to turn, but Ula wrestles the mop away.

Zosia steps back, afraid they will try to hit her with the stick, but now Adela takes a dramatic sniff, her snub nose upturned.

"Oh, that nasty smell makes me have to spit." She crinkles her nose and spits. A blob of spittle lands in Zosia's hair.

"Me too, I can't help it." Ula's spit reaches Zosia's cheek and slides to her neck.

Ula, dangling the mop low, lets it drop to the floor. "Let's go. Come on."

"I don't think Zosia can come; it's still pretty dirty here." As Adela says this, she upturns the pail of brown water upon the just mopped floor. Before it reaches their feet, Ula and Adela rush down the steps.

Zosia weeps as she cleans herself up and remops the landing. She sees, in the floor's shine, her own enraged reflection. She is furious at those girls, and she is furious at herself for not fighting back.

Her hands continue to shake even after she wrings out the mop and dumps the pail, as she stores the supplies in the cleaning closet and makes her way to the music classroom.

Chapter 27

Zosia reaches for the little violin, tightening the bow and tuning the strings the way Sister Nadzieja has taught her. Still shaky, she begins searching for the notes.

All her life she has been hearing them, though she's had to keep them tamped down, muted. Today, reeking of bleach amid school desks dwarfed by walls of cracking white plaster, she hunts. Her fingers clamp, first to this string, then to that one, while her bow rushes in for the test.

One by one, the notes accumulate to take her back, back. She is in the parlor in Gracja, nestled in her grandfather's lap, the sound of her parents' music like the whip-up of dust clouds around manic dancing feet. Vibrant melodies. The wild pluck of strings.

Zosia's own sound comes out alternately scratchy, then airy, and she can't play at all fast. But she sticks with it, and in time she masters a crisper sound, a steady rhythm: the whirring wind.

Her throat tightens and her chest heaves as she sounds out other melodies, songs she composed in her head in the barn, recalling times when her whole family was together:

walking by the riverbank, the water scalloped by a gusting breeze; conversing after dinner, instruments within reach.

Only in *this* music, wistful and defiant, can she find something of her own without giving herself away. Find her family, her home. Shuttered windows. Yellow stars. Notes like these to bridge the shared night.

Chapter 28

Spring 1943

In the woods, the frozen earth begins to thaw. Róża, Miri, and Chana finally break winter camp and begin the journey southward. The icicles that have bearded the trees all winter drip wet and clear. Róża yanks off a long ice tip to suck on as she navigates the thick spring mud.

Róża's boots are still hanging on, wrapped in dirt-caked twine. Because her socks have worn thin at the heels and are stiff with dried blood at the toes, her feet chafe inside her boots, causing her flesh to tear and flap. The cracks in her hands have no chance of healing as they bleed anew with each burrow's digging. Róża wraps herself in her threadbare sweater, its buttons long missing.

All three of them are stained with dirt, their hair matted and itchy from lice, their faces sunken and gaunt, their lips swollen and cracking. As mirrors for one another, they offer no comfort. But the focus is on movement and on food. The thaw coaxes new shoots from the ground and new buds on plants that can be eaten.

Their boots leave tracks in the mud. Each tries what she can to prevent it: Chana wears a pair of socks over her boots;

Róża alters her stride in an effort to obscure the pattern and even walks on all fours at times. Since the soles of Miri's boots have detached completely, she ties them on backward so that her tracks point in the opposite direction.

"Now soldiers will have to split up and search in both directions to find us."

Róża swells with gratitude for their company.

She thought she'd be on her own by now. Chana spoke continually of enlisting in a partisan group. But Miri proved as determined, and eventually, the sisters agreed to accompany Róża as far as the woods' southern edge before searching for a unit. Perhaps Miri's desire to help Róża reunite with Shira has something to do with *her* mother, who fought to save their little brother even as the soldiers brought batons down upon her. Whatever the reasons, Róża is glad they've stuck with her.

Peering at Shira's photograph, a fixture in Róża's hands by firelight, Miri says, "You must get her."

"Yes." Róża takes in her daughter's face, the cream of her cheeks and the almond of her eyes.

Unimpeded by wind and frost, they cover substantial distances. Now Róża's imagination runs. She conjures the convent with thick stone walls and wrought-iron gating. She pictures her arrival there, even muses at the prospect of concealing herself at first, just for a short time, peeking through the gate to glimpse Shira before surprising her. Placing a small gift, perhaps something knitted or sewn, at the edge of the yard just as the children are let out to play and stepping out as Shira finds it and whoops with joy. If only somehow Natan could be there too. He loved Shira's squeals, her full belly laughter. Sounds that Shira was made to stifle and that Róża can hardly remember.

Róża's night terrors recede as they move southward toward Celestyn, as she imagines Shira safe—and soon found. Guided by Natan's old compass, the three women walk together past a train track, its wood ties looted for burning. Miri keeps one hand clasped around Róża's arm. Chana is talking about food again. This time, about eggs.

"Do you know that, for an entire year, I devoted myself to making a new egg dish each day?"

"Hmm?" Róża purses her lips. Miri gives her arm a squeeze. She thinks of her friend Marek's old potato jokes. *Why did the potato cross the road? Because he saw a fork up ahead. What do you say to an angry potato? Anything, just butter him up.*

"It's true," Chana insists. "It required me to learn a lot about French cooking. I made every kind of omelet, custard, soufflé, meringue."

"They were delicious, all three hundred and sixty-five of them," Miri says.

Róża smiles, wondering what kind of beautiful, well-equipped kitchen Chana and Miri must have had. Her family's kitchen was fine—and her mother was a masterful baker—but Róża could never have made such delicacies, certainly not a year's worth of them. She looks from sister to sister, registering for the first time that they'd been *wealthy*.

"Were these 'egg dishes' or just dishes that involved eggs? I mean, could you count a crepe?" Róża asks.

"Yes, why not?"

"What about a simple cake that calls for an egg?"

"No."

"Spring salad?"

"Yes."

Róża can't actually remember the last time she had an

egg of any kind. But she remembers when Shira had them. Róża's mouth pools as she thinks of it and she swallows hard. Her recurring wish: that she'd pocketed some from the coop before she ran from the barn.

Still arm in arm with Miri, Róża feels her boots sink and squelch with every step.

"Mousse?" Miri is now asking.

"Of course!"

"What about challah?"

"I don't think challah counts."

"But a challah takes a lot of eggs."

All three are silent now, remembering. Róża fingers the frosting tip in her pocket.

"Deviled eggs?"

"Kluski?"

For the next several hours, they go on like this. Róża and Miri scour their minds for every egg dish they have heard of, asking if it counted and if Chana made it during her egg year.

They parse *new*: "Could you make a cheese soufflé one day and a mushroom soufflé the next?"

Another arm squeeze from Miri and Róża looks over to see Chana, a vexed expression on her face. At some point they vow that they will steal eggs the next chance they get so that Chana can work her magic, albeit over an open flame.

Night falls and the weather remains mild, the air sweet. A bright moon shining through branches dapples the forest floor, chandelier-like, with droplets of light. Róża looks from one sister to another.

"Let's sleep out in the open, just this once as a special pleasure. Our hands need a break from digging."

However reckless, it feels imperative to Róża to avoid the desolation of sleeping in a makeshift grave. In her burrow, surrounded by dirt and shadowed by branches, doubts creep into her mind: that she may never make it to the convent, may never again see Shira and hold her in her arms.

Miri looks as if she is about to protest, but Chana agrees and Miri stays quiet.

"Good!" Róża exclaims. "Our bed will be under the trees."

Mother Agnieszka told Zosia always to hide in her closet when the Germans come, but tonight there's no warning. Soldiers are already in the stairwells, heading toward the children's room. Zosia sees the terror on Sister Alicja's face as she steers Zosia into a makeshift line—the second roll call required of the children.

A tall, stern-faced soldier paces before them. Zosia clutches the fabric of her nightgown to stop her hands from shaking. She keeps her eyes down, but then the soldier's boots snap together, causing her to startle. She adjusts her gaze straight ahead, fearful, breathing in his scent of starch and cedar and sweat, trying not to stare at the tiny hairs that poke out from his nostrils, the faint mark of an iron upon his shirt collar.

Sister Olga paces behind them just as he paces in front. Sister Olga is the one who in winter suggested the musical instruments be burned for firewood and who just yesterday made Janina kneel on beans for giggling during chores. Zosia wishes she could break out of the line, run to her closet, curl up in her solitary space, however dark and lonely.

At some point the soldier stills, distracted by the cross-stitched linens topping the bureaus. His expression softens as he walks over to look at them. After a few minutes he nods to Sister Olga, and she ushers him toward the stair. The girls shuffle toward their beds.

Adela asks, not quietly, "Why weren't you in the line last time?"

Zosia freezes, fearing the soldier is still in earshot. Are his footsteps on the landing? Was he first heading down the steps, now turning back?

As Zosia stands, unmoving, Adela grabs Zosia's blanket from the corner of her bed, throws it into the air, and catches it. Zosia rushes forward and retrieves it. She buries it deep beneath her bedcovers, thinking of the letters tucked into the seam, spelling out her name.

In bed, Zosia cups her hands even tighter than usual because her bird's bright yellow feathers are puffed out in a flamboyant ruffle. No striated feathers as in her dream; he is healthy and poised to protect her, his piercing eyes trained on Adela. Yet his call is still a two-note tremble.

Zosia makes a quiet clucking noise to soothe him. In her head she speaks admonishing words. *I know that you want to peck at her, but you mustn't, not now with Sister Olga coming back. We'd get in terrible trouble.* When she is sure her bird will stay put, Zosia lets a finger rise to stroke his soft, downy chest. She thinks of the time Ula awoke with a cry, clutching her arm in confusion. Zosia and her bird knew what happened.

Zosia positions herself to be still through the night—shoulders and head lined straight, never tilted to one side—and drifts into sleep. Her dreams go not to Adela or to Ula or to Sister Olga but to a long-ago sunlit room filled with the scents of varnish and wood glue.

Violins are everywhere, scattered among boards of maple and spruce on worktables crowded with glue pots and brushes and chisels and knives. In the center of the room, a man Zosia once knew but can no longer remember sits on a stool, hunched over a violin, his fingers stained the color of cherries. He has a beard that a bird could nest in, bushy and long, and his eyes crinkle up at the edges like a smile even as he complains that, with the high humidity, his varnish is slow to dry.

"How long have you been waiting?" Zosia asks, happy to be standing beside him once again.

He winks. "Do you see this beard? I didn't have it when I applied the first coat."

Zosia asks the man if he might play something for her. He lifts a violin from the wall rack and plays a snippet of Gypsy music. Then he continues his work. He tells her Jesus wished to be a violin maker, so that he might have the joy of creating something not just with his mind and his heart but also with his hands.

A bit later, it is time for her to go. The man kisses Zosia on each cheek and puts his hands palm to palm with hers. But just as he begins folding his long fingers over her short ones, she sees the glare of bayonets coming through their entwined grasp. "Nie—"

Zosia wakes in a sweat. Several girls stare sleepily in her direction, all too used to nightmares. Kasia once again offers her doll. Zosia takes it and swallows hard, unable to blot out her scream's echo.

Chapter 29

When she is summoned to Mother Agnieszka's chamber, Zosia finds a man nearly as old as her grandpa standing beside Sister Nadzieja. His heavy mustache and bushy sideburns give him a downturned look, but his eyes are soft and light, and a black violin case is tucked neatly beneath his arm.

"Zosia," Sister Nadzieja starts, "this is Pan Skrzypczak. He is a real violin instructor, and—"

Mother Agnieszka shifts uncomfortably and cuts in. "As I mentioned, Pan Skrzypczak, our asking you here may have been ill conceived. A teacher of your renown and we have no funds."

"I thought you could play for him," Sister Nadzieja presses on before Pan Skrzypczak can respond to Mother Agnieszka. "Perhaps start with your arpeggios?" She hands Zosia the classroom violin and bow, and Zosia understands: *she* arranged this meeting.

Pan Skrzypczak nods Zosia on. Zosia brings the violin to her chin and plays her arpeggios. As soon as she finishes,

Mother Agnieszka breaks in again. "That was very nice, Zo-sia. Now, Sister Nadzieja, if you will take Zosia back to—"

"Please—wait." Pan Skrzypczak looks apologetically at Mother Agnieszka. Turning to Zosia, he says, "Do you know any songs you could play for me?"

"She knows the beginning of Mazurka *Obertas*," says Sister Nadzieja.

Zosia loves the dramatic start! As she plays, she imagines costumed dancers circling one another, arms hooked, their eyes sparking with each playful pluck of strings. Zosia pulls her bow its full length, back and forth. When the music slows, briefly languid, she imagines an embrace; then speeding up, the flight of feet, raised arms, and twirling skirts; and on an extended note, long and trilling, her bird flitting above the dance, excited and happy.

"That was very good," Pan Skrzypczak says when she finishes midway. "Now, can you copy me?"

Pan Skrzypczak takes out his own violin and plays an array of notes, simple at first, then more and more difficult, with subtle variations in tempo and volume. Zosia matches him exactly each time. They play, back and forth, a long while.

"Pan Skrzypczak, I must apologize for taking up your time—"

"Astonishing."

Zosia flushes warm.

"But we cannot afford—"

"You needn't pay me." He smiles at Zosia. "Twice a week."

"What?" Surprise marks Mother Agnieszka's face.

"I'd like to work twice a week. She must have a better bow. I can get one for her. And she must be given time every day to practice."

"You'd have to teach her here, Pan Skrzypczak. Zosia cannot leave the grounds."

Pan Skrzypczak turns to Mother Agnieszka with another smile. "A teacher lives for a student like her."

Back in her room, Zosia sits on the edge of her bed, her mind a jumble. A real teacher! Once, in a snippet of story she remembers about an enchanted garden, the little girl composed a pastorale for her bird to chirp, alerting a mother deer to a giant's presence. *Now,* Zosia thinks, *I can learn to play it myself!*

Chapter 30

Summer 1943

The girls form a tight circle in the yard, each with a daisy in hand, and take turns playing "He loves me, he loves me not." Each flushes and giggles as the group demands, "*Who?* You have to name the boy before you start, or else it won't be true!" Ula and Adela wear daisy chains as crowns.

Zosia is in the outside corridor, praying they won't notice her as she rushes by, but Adela calls out.

"Zosia, why don't you join us? Oh, but it may not be possible. There would need to be a boy who could love you."

Zosia's bird batters in her sleeve, eager to swoop upon Adela and rip the crown off her head. He wants to send the flower petals into the air like feathers, like shreds of handkerchief squares. But Sister Nadzieja appears.

"You girls should concern yourselves with *God's* love, not boys' love. And it's chore time. Go quickly—before Sister Olga notices that no one is helping in the refectory."

Zosia reaches a finger into her sleeve to pat her bird, but

he nips at her. She swallows a cry. Sister Nadzieja looks over at her, kindly.

Zosia wonders if Sister Nadzieja feels frightened by Sister Olga too.

If she wishes, she could play the girls' games.

If there is someone else, other than God, whose love she longs for.

Róża and Miri venture out to gather mushrooms, minding how they move through the woods, pulling their feet back with each step as Henryk instructed Róża, weaving through the vegetation in strides that defy patterning. They discover cloudberries and greedily add handfuls to their harvest. They return to the fire to find Chana presiding over a soup. When they present their yield, she looks disappointed at the mushrooms.

"Just the kurki?"

Róża and Miri exchange looks.

"I can make a much better soup with a different variety. Didn't you see any boletus, near the fallen tree trunk?"

"Chana, the soup you make with these will be fine. It's too dangerous to go back."

"It would have a richer flavor."

"I'm sure it will be delicious as it is."

"Nothing we eat is delicious."

"It will be fine. Thank you for making it."

Chana's food obsession extends to everything. She reminisces about favorite meals and recipes and ingredients—not just eggs. Even when the conversation has nothing to do with food she manages a reference, as if it's not painful—let alone annoying—to think about delicacies when they're starving. In response to a distracted stare she asks, "*What*, are you thinking of blue almonds?" so that for the next hours, all three dream of almonds—whatever color—longing for their crisp, salty crunch.

On a morning that dawns clear and bright, their walking leads them to a stream. They take long drinks, then splash their faces. They have been sleeping aboveground, enjoying the open air and the restored sense of humanity that comes from not burrowing down like moles.

"Why don't we wash everything?" Chana asks. "My pants are so stiff I can barely walk in them."

"And my hair, I'll do anything to stop itching for a few minutes!" Miri exclaims.

The relief of the cold water on Róża's sore, blistered feet travels through her whole body as she takes her first tentative steps into the stream. She bends to submerge her arms; she catches water in the cups of her hands to pour on the back of her neck.

They take turns bathing and scrubbing their clothes. They dunk their heads and pick the lice from one another's scalps. Afterward, they put on the dry things they have: Chana wears the pants she took from the man killed for testing Jewish. Miri and Róża put on the skirts they nabbed from a clothes-line during a food raid nearer the perimeter. All three wear damp undershirts, cool against their skin.

Róża hangs her pants on a tree branch and returns to their site. Before she doused them, mud caked and lice infested, into the stream, she unstitched the convent ad-dress card and placed it—she's sure of it—inside her left boot. But now she can't find it, not inside either of her boots or anywhere nearby. It's not tucked into the sleeve of her sweater or beneath the cook pot either, and though she *knows* the address—she made up that story to help her memorize it and she has never forgotten it, not a single detail—the loss of the card feels like the loss of Shira herself, all over again. She rushes, frantic, along the edge of the stream, peering to see if the card is in the water.

Chana watches her, unmoved, mumbling something about how losing an engagement band doesn't mean the couple is not engaged.

"What are you talking about?"

"I'm just saying, you don't need the card if you know the address. It's actually safer that you don't have it."

Chana intends this to comfort Róża, but instead it alarms her further. If the card is not in her possession, it's somewhere in the woods. It could be found by soldiers; it could lead them straight to Shira!

Róża looks through the clothes again, then riffles around near the pot. She doesn't take care with the noise she's making. Her hair, wet now with tears, sticks stiffly to her cheeks.

"Róża, here!"

Róża looks up to see Miri holding the card, drenched and muddy, in her extended hand. All this time, Miri had been carefully retracing Róża's steps, searching under branches, among piles of leaves.

"Oh!" Róża runs toward her, reaching for the card. "How can I ever thank you?"

Something in Miri's expression reminds Róża of her father. She thinks of the long-ago time she went to him, fearful and guilty, when she accidentally broke her mother's favorite bowl. Her father reassured her in his steady way. "It's all right, Różyczka, we'll gather all the shards and fix it right up." As if he understood life itself to be the holding together of small broken pieces.

Róża wakes before dawn to the rumble of tanks, the distant sound of boots tromping the ground. In an instant, she is up on her feet, heart pounding.

"Miri, Chana, wake up!"

The reverberations come from every direction. Róża is sure that soldiers are circling the vicinity. *Why did I ever suggest we sleep aboveground? And worse, how could we have let it become our habit?*

As the ground shakes, she searches for cover. A thick, fallen tree trunk. Scattered branches. If they can dig out a hollow by the tree's side, they can all three burrow against it.

Róża digs as quickly as she can. The sisters spring to action, digging alongside her. Their arms work spastically, driven by panic as their breath grows more and more shallow. Never before during their time in the woods have they dug harder or faster. The hole expands, but not quickly enough. It looks big enough to fit two bodies, not three. They hear the soldiers coming closer.

"It'll do," Miri says. "Climb in and I'll get cover."

Róża and Chana climb in as Miri grabs armfuls of pine branches. She drags them over the hole and spreads them, concealing Róża and Chana.

"What are you doing, Miri? Get in," Chana whispers.

But only Miri's hand pokes through to squeeze Chana's arm.

And then she is sprinting away through the trees. Chana's

eyes, confused at first, now fill with horror. Again and again, she shakes her head no. *No!* Róża takes Chana's hands in hers and strains to hear above the pounding boots, the quaking earth.

A single gunshot.

Chana throws off the branches and starts to climb out of the burrow, but Róża pulls her back and thrusts the branches over them once again. She wraps one arm around Chana's face to muffle her wails and presses hard against her torso to immobilize her. They must wait now. Even if Miri led the soldiers in the opposite direction, it's likely they will be back, hoping for more bounty.

Róża's mouth fills with the tastes of metal and salt, and it takes her several seconds to realize: she has bitten the inside of her cheek and her tears are coming in through her open mouth. Chana is limp in her arms now.

Pressed against the dug earth, Róża feels a seeping dampness spread across her buttocks, her thighs. The root clippers, stuffed in her pocket, press sharply against her hip bone. Her lips move in Hebrew, the prayers her mother painstakingly taught her.

She strains to see through the branches, to listen for the sound of boots, of dogs. She is desperate to know what's happening, but she doesn't dare move. Time stalls. She hears only the hammering of her heart.

Was it possible that the soldiers left the area, satisfied? Róża listens but hears no sound. She thinks of Miri, how they need to get to her. If there is any chance—

Róża untangles an arm and reaches above her, shifting the branches just enough to see out. She extricates herself and tugs on Chana, tries to pull her from the hole. But Chana is dead weight, curled up, crumpled.

"We need to find her. I'm going to cover you and go look for her."

Róża moves quickly in the direction she thought she heard the shot. Her stomach knots with dread as she traverses the woods, scanning the ground in all directions. The air is damp and misty. The earth sucks at her boots and sticks crackle beneath her weight. Otherwise, it is silent.

She finds Miri facedown in mud, blood mushrooming at the side of her head. Róża drops to her knees. Turning Miri over, Róża finds the trowel she used for digging their hole.

Róża takes hold of Miri's chilled hand and speaks the kaddish, her voice trembling.

Yitgadal v'yitkadash sh'mei raba.
B'alma di v'ra chirutei,
v'yamlich malchutei,
b'chayeichon uv'yomeichon
uv'chayei d'chol beit Yisrael . . .

She sits for a long time before she surveys the ground for digging. She can't imagine carrying Miri back through the woods, burying her in *that* hole—the one that didn't hold her too. She starts on a new hole, sparing Chana the preparation of a burial site.

She cries as she digs, thinking she never had the chance to bury her parents or Natan. And *who knows* about Shira, how she is really doing at the orphanage?

She cuts at the soil and hurls it in heaps. It gives way as the frozen ground did not the night she set to covering the barn rabbit, its blood mixed with hers and what life, stopped short, had started inside her.

When she hears mud squelching, she turns to see Chana approaching, face contorted, legs buckling. Róża scrambles to her feet and rushes toward her, but Chana passes her by and lands on Miri, head upon her chest.

Róża tears at the collar of her shirt until it rips. Chana stands and makes a rip in her shirt, too, rending the left collar above her heart.

When it is time to put Miri in the grave, Chana holds her sister from beneath the shoulders and Róża takes her legs. Rather than drop her into the hole, they sidestep together down into it, still keeping hold of her, and kneel low before letting her go. They grasp piles of soil with their fingers and place it on top of her, covering her legs and torso. Gently, Róża rotates Miri's face to the side before placing dirt over her neck, her cheek, her ear.

They cover Miri slowly, handful by handful of loose earth. Neither can bear to hear even a *plunk*, the ground's weight upon her. Róża's feet and calves get buried too. For several minutes she stays planted there, squatting beside Miri, before she slowly dislodges one foot and the other and climbs out.

Chapter 31

Autumn 1943

The lessons Pan Skrzypczak gives Zosia in Mother Agnieszka's private chambers are the highlight of Zosia's week. She counts the days, then hours, to their appointed meeting times, and she practices every free moment she can. Scales, études, trills, and every shifting and bowing exercise he gives her. When she plays her arpeggios, she focuses on the accuracy of the notes rather than on the endless repetition, trying her hardest to achieve richness of tone with every stroke.

Sometimes Pan Skrzypczak plays along with Zosia in a duet, and she thrills at the harmonies they create together. Other times he keeps his violin tucked beneath his arm and taps a foot or bobs his head, causing his sideburns to puff and billow; or he places his fingers over Zosia's to guide her bow. Zosia likes how he smells of rosin and pipe tobacco; how he listens with his head cocked slightly to the left; how he teaches her pieces by Bartók and Bloch and also Sarasate, music that reminds her of her family in Gracja.

At one lesson, Pan Skrzypczak asks Zosia if she is wearing her hair a different way. Sister Alicja had re-dyed her hair and eyebrows the previous night. Unsure of what to say, Zosia mutters, "I don't think so"; then she tells a story that her mother told her, about Joachim's friends and the music they wrote for him.

"Yes, Joachim's devotion to music was paramount."

Zosia thinks of the other stories her mother told her: the little girl's adventures in the enchanted garden, the invisible daisy chain, the promise that she'd come back for her. None of them true.

Pan Skrzypczak looks as if he could read her thoughts.

"Joachim's motto may have been 'Free but lonesome,' but I think his friends' musical gifts made him feel less alone. Why don't I teach you the Brahms?"

"I already—" She almost tells him how her mother hummed Brahms's Scherzo for her in the barn and even wrote down the first bars. But she stops herself. She promised not to say anything about the past. Yet again, he seems to know.

"Maybe you're familiar with it already?" In his crinkly smile Zosia recognizes that he feels pride in her. Shyly she returns his smile and nods. "You'll learn it even more quickly, then."

At the start of her next lesson, Pan Skrzypczak takes coins from his pocket and hands Zosia a particularly shiny one. On one side, a crowned eagle inside the words *Rzeczpospolita Polska 1938*; on the other side, *1 grosz*, decorated with floral curls. The last time Zosia saw coins of any kind, her mother was sewing them into her jacket lining. She remembers being surprised when they didn't jangle. Zosia can't think where that jacket is now.

"Do you know what I do to practice as best I can?"

Zosia waits to learn.

"I put five coins, just like that, to one side of a table and I play the part I'm working on. If I play it the first time through without mistakes, I move the first coin over. Then I play it a second time; and if again I play it without mistakes, I move the second coin over. However, if I make any mistake at all, *both* coins go back! And so on. When I have four coins moved over, the pressure is really on, because with the next playing, I'm either finished, or *all* the coins go back and I have to start over."

Zosia is eager to follow her teacher's suggestion.

"You can hold on to these coins for your practice sessions. They'll remind you of how important it is to me that you continue with your playing."

As she works through the lesson, trying her very best, Zosia keeps her eyes on the single most curious thing in the austere space—a white crocheted doily on Mother Agnieszka's desk, perhaps a memento of *her* mother?—and doesn't ask her teacher the questions she wants to ask: Does he have a daughter, a family? Even as the pads of her fingers grow calloused and her shoulder starts to ache, Zosia continues to play. She wishes to be good, to be great. She doesn't say it aloud, but she wishes to play in concert halls all around the world, with recordings on the radio like those her grandfather listened to while he worked, so that anyone who tunes in to the broadcast will hear her.

Pan Skrzypczak tasks Zosia hard, but after their lessons, he reveals a more lighthearted side. One afternoon he asks, "Have you ever heard the *Mousetrap* Concerto?"

"No."

"Ah, listen carefully."

Just two short sounds—squeak, thump!—issue from Pan Skrzypczak's violin: the squeak he makes by running the bow upon the strings behind the bridge, and the thump he makes by tapping the top of the violin. It's such a quick "concerto"—poor mouse!—Zosia bursts out laughing. After that, he shows her how to make all sorts of animal sounds with her violin: a cow's moo, a lamb's bleat, a chicken's cluck, a donkey's bray.

Another afternoon, he tells her the story of a recital he'd prepared for as a young student.

"I was very nervous because I was to play my teacher's own composition, which was terribly complicated. The recital was held in a mansion house, with a banquet beforehand for which I had no appetite. *All* I wanted was to warm up my violin and practice! As soon as I could reasonably leave the table, I made my way to a practice room. I had to walk through a winding maze of corridors, not unlike the walkways of this convent. When I finally got settled and began to practice, I found that I didn't remember how the piece was to start. I knew every note after the first measure, but as for the beginning—my mind was an utter blank! So I weaved my way back through the maze to the banquet room. My teacher was still lounging at the table, talking to friends and colleagues, and drinking. I whispered my problem to him.

"'Go back and practice some more. It will come to you,' he said, and waved me away.

"So I weaved my way back to the practice room and picked up my violin to start. But again, I had no memory of the first notes. I went a second time to my teacher.

"'*Please*—my recital is in less than an hour!'

"'All right, all right,' he grumbled, and he left the table

and walked with me through the twists and turns of the halls, to the practice room.

"When he picked up his violin, he played something entirely unfamiliar, a wild improvisation as far as I could tell. It was then that I realized: *He*—my great teacher and renowned composer—didn't remember the start of his piece, either!"

Zosia looks shocked. "What did you do? What did you play at the recital?"

"I improvised my own first measure! I joined it to the rest of the piece as best I could, and kept going."

Today, Pan Skrzypczak is far quieter after the lesson as he pulls a sheet of paper from his briefcase.

"I wrote out a folk song you might know."

He hands Zosia a piece of composition paper filled with notes drawn in thin pencil. Sight-reading as she can, it conjures the dance of light on her red-and-white-stitched bed quilt; the cinnamon-sugar smell of mandelbrot wafting in from the kitchen. "Oh," she exclaims, "my grandmother always hummed this while she did her Friday baking!"

As soon as the words are out of her mouth, Zosia looks up anxiously. Her teacher's expression holds pure kindness in it, but she floods with fear.

Revealing details of her past even to Pan Skrzypczak, who supports her in what she loves, feels threatening.

"I'm sorry, thank you," she says in a jumbled rush, and, paper in hand, she runs to her hiding closet and curls up in the front compartment among the robes. After several minutes, hands still shaking but her breathing calmed, she peers at the music page. In its notes she hears her grandmother's voice, the interwoven sounds of her mama's cello, her *tata*'s violin.

Through tears Zosia sees that with the title space left blank, it appears as an entirely nondescript piece of sheet music. No danger in it.

Zosia vows that, next lesson, she will express her heartfelt thanks to her teacher.

Chapter 32

Soldiers arrive at the convent in the middle of the night to search the children's rooms. Zosia is unsure where to go—to her hiding closet? or into the line with the other girls?—until Sister Alicja swoops in and rushes her to the lavatory, where, in the window glass, illuminated by a single bulb, Zosia sees the reflection of her hair, newly dark at the crown, white to the tips.

Sister Olga can be heard pacing up and down the line, shushing the children. Zosia is terrified that Adela will once again ask why she isn't in line. A loud clatter ensues as bureau drawers are opened and shut, possessions turned out from trunks. Then a strangled silence—a moment in which Zosia remembers waiting for her mother's hands to fold over hers—before Mother Agnieszka's voice, alarm overlaid by a pronounced steadiness, dismisses Sister Olga to her chamber and summons the soldier into the corridor, away from the line of children, close to the lavatory. Sister Alicja stiffens upon hearing the soldier just on the other side of the door, speaking about a discrepancy in ration cards. Zosia's thoughts still fix on Adela: perhaps she won't have a chance to say anything now?

"Why is there an extra bed?"

"I beg your pardon?" Mother Agnieszka asks.

"I counted eighteen beds but only seventeen children."

Sister Alicja's face blanches white. Zosia feels a rising panic. Mother Agnieszka's voice, when it comes, is a pitch higher.

"One of our little girls has typhus, poor dear. I can take you to the infirmary to see her if you'd like."

"*No*—that won't be necessary."

"Very well. Herr Kommandant, I beg of you, these late night raids frighten the chil—" Mother Agnieszka's plea is lost to a pounding of boots on the front stair.

Sister Alicja gathers Zosia and bounds through the lavatory's back door—the nuns' entry, forbidden to the children—before soldiers can barge through the front. Down the nuns' corridor, Alicja slips them into a small side room packed with spare sewing machines. She tugs open a wardrobe, covers Zosia over with the stiff brown fabric of habits, and shuts her in until—after offering watery coffee, but coffee nonetheless, to the soldiers upon their departure—she returns to usher Zosia back through the two lavatory doors, into the quiet dark of the children's room.

Zosia, a knotted pounding in her chest that will linger for hours after, prays for the end of roll call lines.

For the next several weeks, there is less to eat for everyone. The children complain of hunger and the sisters preach piety in suffering—except for Sister Alicja, who complains, too, and is made to fast—until bombs explode nearby, causing them all to forget their stomachs. Zosia overhears the nuns speak of Red Army advances in Ukraine—snatches from Mother Agnieszka's wireless radio. But none of this seems to matter here in Celestyn. Sirens wail ceaselessly. The children practice drills. They walk in hurried lines to the cellar rooms and squeeze to fit within door frames. They dive under their beds when shellings shake the ground.

Once, Adela dives under Zosia's bed. Zosia twists and wiggles to position herself at the opposite end, but Adela says, "I see you. I see everything."

Zosia looks away, quavering. At snack time, Adela demands Zosia's piece of bread and Zosia gives it to her, that day and each day following.

Zosia finds refuge from Adela's tormenting in her lessons with Pan Skrzypczak—and in Kasia's friendship. Once, when Zosia arrived late for her laundry chore—she was supposed to be folding bedsheets, not playing violin, and she was frantic that she'd be punished—she found that Kasia had managed the whole job without her and had even covered for her with Sister Olga by saying she was at a different chore with Sister Nadzieja.

On the day that Kasia tore an altar cloth, Zosia repaired it, trying her best to replicate the close, even, nearly invisible stitches she'd seen her mother make. Kasia thanked Zosia by nabbing two pairs of wool socks from the knit bin and teaching her to "skate" on the slippery, just polished floors. As they careened past the low corridor wall, Kasia spotted two stray cats huddled inside the convent gate. She stopped abruptly, Zosia nearly crashing into her, and observed them for several seconds while catching her breath.

"Who do you think they look like?"

"Hmm?"

"I think the littler one looks like Sister Nadzieja. And the bigger one—see how her paws move as if kneading dough—like Sister Halina."

Zosia giggled to be imagining the cats in dark habits with headdresses tucked around their ears, teaching lessons and baking bread.

Now, they check on the cats daily, and while walking to evening prayers they name what they see in the clouds: an angel with feathery wings, a dragon's head, mashed potatoes, a dollop of cream. They whisper—or, in the case of food likenesses, moan—and if one of them laughs, the other squeezes her hand. They bite their tongues and bow their heads and rush along.

They cover for each other if one drifts back to sleep after morning call, or dallies too long outside, or needs the washing done quickly to remove a careless stain. But there is no cover for Zosia the day Sister Olga takes it upon herself to inspect the children's room. Her stomach churns with dread as the nun brusquely opens the tops of the trunks and lifts the mattresses to expose what's been tucked beneath: two uncooked potatoes wrapped in a napkin.

"Zosia, come over here right now. Explain this—"

"It is food that I saved." Zosia rushes over; she wants to put it back where she'd stowed it, but Sister Olga holds it up high, out of her reach.

"I can see perfectly well that it is food. How dare you save food for yourself when we are all going hungry?"

"It's not for me. It's for my mother, in case—" She grasps for it.

"For your mother? What a hideous lie!"

"It is not! If she comes for me, I—"

"You must be punished for this. I'll do it myself." Sister Olga takes Zosia's arm and shoves her toward her bed.

Zosia begins to cry. She can feel the eyes of the other girls on her.

"Stop your crying. You are a bad child. You deserve this."

In the corner of the room, there is a long wooden ruler used for taking the heights of the children. Sister Olga grabs it, brings it down hard upon Zosia's outstretched hands once, twice, three times. A stinging, burning pain rises—along with the despairing thought that it may take days before she will be able to play her violin.

Zosia crumples onto her bed. Kasia runs to her side but steps back when Sister Alicja rushes in.

"Zosia, what happened?"

"I hid food under my bed. But it wasn't for me!"

"Oh, Zosia."

"I wanted to have it for my mama when she came for me. Sister Olga took it away. And she punished me." Her face contorts.

"Now, now. We can get more. You are a good girl, Zosia." Sister Alicja strokes her hair, moving it away from her face.

"No. I am not. I'm bad just like Sister Olga said."

Ever since the priest's Epiphany homily, she's felt stained. But it's remembering what she did in the barn—tapping and chirping when she was meant to be silent and gobbling Krystyna's treats while her mother starved—that shames her most. She can't take a bite of food anymore without thinking about it. Only stowing little bits from her meals, bread crusts and potatoes, makes her feel better.

"Zosia, let me take a look at those hands of yours."

Zosia hears a catch in Sister Alicja's voice as she looks at her fingers, swollen and already bruising.

"Stay still now, you hear me? I'll be right back with Sister Nadzieja. The two of us will get you fixed up."

Zosia nuzzles her shred of blanket with her cheek and stares up at the high rectangular window, the drifting clouds. Kasia steps close and reaches for her arm.

Róża shuffles straight legged to minimize the sound of her movements in the woods. The leaves, high in the branches and full of color just a week ago, are gone from the trees. Winds have swept the trees bare, the remains of autumn delivered to the forest floor, dried and curled, a thick carpet announcing her every step with a riot of rustling. Chana, wearily oblivious, lets herself get whisked along.

Róża remembers how, on their journey out of Gracja, Shira hummed and tapped and asked endless questions and called for her *tata*. For better or worse, Chana makes no sound at all. Róża fears Chana is close to starving, rawboned and torpid. Even when they manage to find food—as when Róża found chanterelles to boil into a soup—Chana barely eats.

Burdened with keeping them both alive, Róża flares with frustration, then regret. She knows that Chana is privately cataloging her own missteps: how she drowned out Miri's grief with her anger; how she allowed her partisan dreams to push them to the periphery of the woods. Her actions conceived at the time as protective; in truth they were protective of her*self*.

Róża understands this form of torture.

A cold rain streaks the white sky. Zosia quavers in front of the classroom's open window. She lowers her bruised, shaking hand to the sill. Her bird perches on her forefinger.

"I'm going to miss you terribly, but you must fly as quickly as you can to the barn and tell Mama I need her. She'll follow you, I know she will. Watch out for soldiers, and others too. Find the safest route and lead her back to me, *please*!"

The bird hops from Zosia's finger to the open window casement, then flies off. Zosia watches until the streak of yellow disappears into the white.

A worry sets in, that her mother won't recognize his tremulous two-note call. She must pray that he will regain his eighteen-note song along the way. She walks to the chapel and drops into a pew, her throbbing hands cupped in her lap.

Chapter 33

Pan Skrzypczak arrives for Zosia's next lesson but Zosia refuses to take her hands from her pockets.

"Begin at once with your tuning. I expect you to be prepared and ready when I arrive here."

She digs her hands deeper, clenching the fabric of her dress.

Pan Skrzypczak pauses in his own tuning and looks at Zosia more closely. "What's the matter? I've never seen you not want to play."

Zosia blinks back tears. How can he—her beloved teacher—not understand? "I *do* want to play. I always want to—"

"Well then?"

Slowly she brings out her hands, splotched purple and swollen around the knuckles, for him to see.

"Oh—"

Zosia fears he is going to ask her what happened, but he doesn't. He just takes a long breath and exhales.

"How about *I* play for *you* today? It will be good for you to hear the *Baal Shem* played in its entirety."

Zosia nods, flooding with relief.

"You can sit in this chair, I don't think Mother Agnieszka will mind. But first, have I ever told you about the time, as a boy, I nearly broke a finger playing ball and this just before a recital?"

Chapter 34

Winter 1944

Chana looks to be glazed over, but her legs still move beneath her. The day is colder than any Róża has known, and barren, deserted even of birds. Every bit of exposed skin bites: the tip of her nose, the area around her eyes, the top of her left wrist where her glove and coat sleeve gap. There is no fresh snow. Without cover, their boots leave prints. Róża focuses on varying her steps as she leads Chana toward the center of the forest, hoping to find something to forage.

When a man steps out from behind a tree, rifle in hand, Róża jerks back, nearly slipping. She reaches into her pocket, fingers searching for the cyanide pill, but then she sees that he is not a German. That's clear from his ragged coat, his ravaged boots.

"Wait," the man commands, and steps closer, staring at Chana.

Róża pushes Chana behind her in a vain effort at protection.

But Chana stares back, brow furrowed, squinting as if to narrow her vision to a single point.

"Hershel?" she rasps in a near-silent whisper.

Róża whips her head around.

The man stares even more concertedly, still unable to place her.

"It's me, Chana. From Warsaw." Chana's cracked voice comes from a different lifetime. For the first time in weeks, her eyes clear and her body shivers as if only now it feels the cold.

Róża looks back and forth between them.

Something registers in the man's eyes. "Chana. I can't believe this," he is saying.

The unlikelihood of their meeting, but also, Róża thinks, Chana's radically altered appearance.

"The last I saw you, you were training for a chess tournament," Chana says.

"And now I am a patrol guard."

"A patrol guard?" Róża asks. She's wondering, *Is he part of an army unit?*

"Our camp is just down there." He points with his rifle, and now, several log structures come into view.

They stare dumbstruck at the scene around them as Hershel escorts them to a fire to get warm. At one end, there are dugouts built into the ground, their roofs packed with dirt and branches. Inside are wooden bunks topped with straw. Beyond the dugouts, lean-to spaces form a row. In one, there is a working tailor; in another, a shoemaker. Beyond these, there is a leather workshop with saddles, stolen from villagers, stacked in its corners, and a metal shop. Róża gapes. People walk about with guns slung across their backs. The camp is *protected* and even somewhat informed: A news scout, using a rejiggered radio, hears of Allied bombings in Berlin and spreads the report.

Róża had struggled terribly getting Chana to part from Miri's burial site, and for the past months, as Chana nearly gave up in grief, she alone bore the major tasks of their survival: gathering wood, clipping roots, digging burrows. Now she looks upon this miniature "village" replete with shelters, a bake house, a medical clinic. This place where, together, many share the burden of survival.

Part partisan camp, part family camp, frail men and women shuffle amid young, able-bodied soldiers. There is a liveliness here Róża hasn't seen in years, and she inhales, practically gulps it. She squeezes Chana's hand. Hadn't Miri heard there was such a place? She had suggested they come, the first day they'd met.

Chana, also enlivened, has explained to Róża that Hershel was in the class ahead of her in school, that he was a chess champion.

Hershel, who had stepped away, returns with two hunks of bread, a shy smile on his face. "I have to get back to my post. I brought this for you to eat. Not too fast, or it won't stay down." His eyes fix on Chana. "I will find you when my shift is over."

A hammering sound draws their attention toward the metal shop. The air reeks of sulfur. Gun parts and bullets lie scattered everywhere: supplies for resistance fighters. Róża turns to see if Chana has noticed the heap of weapons, but another sight—some activity across the square—stops her.

Children. They flock out of the schoolhouse, arms outstretched, and gather in their mothers' skirts. The mothers, a congregation in wait, kneel down and absorb their small sons and daughters, snuggling them and raising them up, even as they balance other, littler children in their arms.

Róża loses her own balance.

"Róża?"

She feels Chana's tug on her hand, hears the call of her name. But she can't turn away.

Here are mothers, in the woods, in winter, who did not part from their children. They kept them with them, and together they survived. It had been possible—

The sun fades quickly and crowds of people cluster around the campfire. Everywhere Róża looks, she notices little girls. Skin the color of apricots, hands sticky with pine sap. One calls out, "Mama!"

Chana is speaking to someone who points out the sleeping bunks and the cook's quarters. Róża interrupts.

"I don't want to stay here. Chana, I can't—"

"Róża. Please." Life glimmers in Chana's eyes for the first time since Miri died.

Róża curls into herself and sobs.

Chana learns of a bath basin where there is heated kettle water, real soap, and several combs, even tightly grooved ones to help remove lice. She leads Róża there. Róża yields to the warm water washing over her exhausted, battered body and sits, compliant, as Chana combs through her hair section by section, the tines running over her scalp, close at the nape of her neck, and down her back.

"This comb is probably the camp's most valuable possession."

Róża looks at it and floods with regret as she thinks of the lice that infested Shira's hair despite the constant braiding;

the spiking fever that nearly claimed her life. Róża couldn't keep her safe *or* near.

"Let's wrap you dry and get you to bed."

Róża drops into the underground bunk she is directed to and sleeps. She doesn't leave the dugout for two days straight. Chana, assigned to be the cook's assistant, brings her food and tries to coax her outside.

"Please, we don't have to live in hiding here."

There is a glow in Chana's face, visible even in the dim light given off by saturated strips of smoldering pine bark. Róża closes her eyes. She is certain she saw a girl Shira's age in the camp, running, playing chase. Her longing pierces as it did when she first left the barn.

When Róża wakes next, hours later, she is unsure whether it is day or night. The dank underground space feels close and tight around her now. She gets up and moves through the shadows, her hands feeling for the earthen walls, her feet venturing short, tentative steps until she grips the ladder rail. She shoves aside the branches overhead and pulls herself out from the darkness.

She shivers in the bracing air. It is night, yet the sky is lighter than the underground, and she has to blink several times before her sight adjusts. Camp flames strut. Music, spirited and soulful, floats into the night: the sound of fiddles, flutes, and a dulcimer. It reminds Róża of the music she and Natan played; Shira padding into the parlor, her hair still damp from bath time, settling into a grandparent's lap to listen.

She picks her way along the path, slick and patchy, to find that the people circling the fire are adults. The children put to bed, thank God.

Men and women cluster, speaking in low tones. Young couples snuggle close, no words at all. Sharing a bottle between them, four Soviet partisans huddle with fighters to discuss an upcoming mission, then break for their camp, west of here.

Róża does not want to camp with these families. She wants to warm up by the fire and find Chana to discuss leaving; her aim hasn't changed. She still must reach the forest border near Celestyn so that she can be ready, as soon as it's safe, to reclaim Shira.

Chana isn't around the fire. Róża thinks to seek her out at Hershel's post, or else return to her bunk until morning when they can start off fresh. But a man she saw earlier in the metal shop strides toward her. His eyes peek out, amber, from beneath tufts of shaggy, unkempt hair. He is nearly a head taller than her.

"Tell me your name."

His directness startles her. She pulls her coat tightly around her. "Róża."

"Różyczka!"

At hearing him say her name in the diminutive—her childhood name—Róża looks up, and a smile crosses her face before any thought can stifle it. "And yours?"

"Aron."

Aron tells Róża that he studied mechanical engineering. When the war broke out, he came to the forest to fight. He repairs weapons between missions.

"Missions for what?" Despite a desire to retreat, she is drawn by a brightness in him that scruff and grime can't dim. She thinks of her own appearance. Before the war, she was considered a beauty, with her dark blue eyes set against her curled hair, her fine-boned features and willowy form. Now she is gaunt and pale, dressed in her ragged clothes despite finally being clean. If Aron notices her shirt, rent in mourning, he doesn't mention it.

"For our survival. Food—and warfare," he answers.

An organizer within the camp strides over, interrupting. "I need to know what work you will do here."

"Róża, meet Sonia," Aron says. "Sonia, Róża."

"I'm not sure we will stay."

"Not stay?" This is Aron.

"Everyone works," Sonia insists.

"Yes, well. I used to help in my mother's bakery. But—"

"Can you sew?"

"Yes."

"Excellent. Go see Shmuel, the tailor, first thing in the morning; he's in charge of that."

Aron nods as if it's settled. Róża thinks back to the first time she met Natan, the day he came to her father's workshop for a violin repair. He poked his head into the parlor where Róża was playing her cello and asked, almost reverently, if she'd like to work on duets with him.

"I should return to my bunk," Róża says.

In the morning, Róża finds Shmuel hunched over an actual pedal-pump sewing machine. The camp is filled with such unlikely objects. Tree saws. Blacksmith tools. A woodstove. All stolen, Róża guesses, and lugged to the camp. The foot pedal needs greasing; it gives off the smell of burnt hair with each push.

"I'm Róża. Sonia sent me to help you with sewing this morning."

"Good, I can use the help. There is a mission in a few days' time, and the fighters need their belts to actually hold bullets."

Róża settles herself at a small table and gets to work, reinforcing the stitches on the belts, as many as she can, paying careful attention so that not a single bullet will slip out. After a time, Róża loses herself in the rhythm—Shmuel's press of the pedal, the yank and tug of thread through fabric—and her mind goes to the outfits she crocheted for Shira's make-believe bird and the all-too-real letters she stitched into her blanket seam.

When Shmuel looks up from his work, he frowns to see Róża shiver. "I have an extra jacket in that bin over there if you're cold."

"It's not that. But thank you."

Across the square, Róża sees a mother bounce her child, hold her close.

At mealtime, Róża stands in a long line for soup. People around her grouse that it's beets and potatoes once again. Róża tastes it, creamy and thick, before leaving the line. She cannot believe how good it is.

"What's *in* this?" Róża asks. Its richness causes her to shudder with pleasure.

"Milk." The young woman who ladles the soup looks prideful.

"Milk!" Róża can't think of the last time she had milk! She can think only of the burnt roots and mushrooms that she and Chana have eaten for the last several months.

"Two days ago," the woman continues, "Itzhak returned from the countryside with a pail of milk. Liquid gold, kept on ice. We've taken to guarding it."

There are potatoes, too, and salt.

Róża looks around and wonders whether the upcoming mission is for food or warfare. A man named Alter paces the camp's perimeter, gripping a wooden gun—a carving, not a real weapon to grant him a place among the fighters—and mumbles to himself. She spots Chana seated beside Hershel, talking and eating. Róża occupies a solitary rock. She eats quietly, greedily, turned away from the gathering families.

Later in the day, Aron steps into the sewing shop and stands before Róża.

"I've been looking for you! Do you want to take a little walk? Shmuele, can you spare her for a bit?" Before either can answer, he says, "Good, we'll leave in a few minutes. I'll come for you."

Shmuel smiles at Róża and resumes his work. "Clever, that one. Devised a mechanical chair for his father when sores ravaged his feet and legs. Apparently the chair even operated on the cobbles of the Białystok ghetto, until German soldiers made a game of shooting at it."

Róża thinks that Aron is as pushy as he is clever. She'd prefer to keep busy with a useful job rather than walk with him.

But then Aron returns carrying a pair of well-sized boots with rubber soles. To feel soft padding at the base of her heels and in the cup of her toes, no chafing, no biting soreness along the tops of her feet, Róża could cry.

"Won't you come?"

Aron leads the way through a stand of birches and down a hill, making no effort to conceal his tracks. Close up, he smells of bullets and jerky. After a few minutes, they arrive at a stream. Aron motions to a thick toppled tree, a bench to sit on while watching the water wend through the snow—a scene of quiet, saving beauty. As Róża settles, Aron reaches into his satchel to reveal a pear.

"Oh! Where did you get it?"

Aron just smiles and hands it to her. She takes a bite—grainy, sweet, and full of light.

"It's the best thing I've ever eaten."

They sit on the tree trunk and pass the pear back and forth, Aron taking smaller and smaller nibbles so as to ensure that Róża has the last bite.

When they get back to the camp, Róża senses excitement in the air.

"What's going on?"

"Soon it will be Shabbas."

Shabbas. Róża had long ago lost track of the days of the week. She marked the passing of time first by nicks in the barn rafter, then by knots on a string. The last time Róża observed Shabbas, her parents and Natan were alive. Shira had watched wide-eyed as her grandmother, with closed eyes, summoned the flames.

Róża doesn't speak of it to Aron. She can't speak of what came *before*.

"Thank you for the walk. I enjoyed it."

"Me too, Różyczka."

At sunset a loaf of challah materializes, as does a pair of candles in tarnished candlesticks. Little girls walk past with baskets of bite-size bread slices piled aloft. As she speaks out the prayers Róża aches for her family, to have them standing by her side. *They are in a better place. They aren't suffering. The anguish will get easier.* She utters the ancient holy words and she tells herself these things, trying to believe them.

Mission preparations ramp up, with seven men and women readying to leave. Aron is among them. People check munitions, pack food into sacks, fill canteens with water. Róża and Shmuel inspect the restitched bandoliers one last time before handing them out.

"How long will they go for?" Róża asks.

"However long it takes."

When Aron enters the shop, he slings two of the belts crosswise over his shoulders. A little boy named Paweł, dark curls down his back, trails him, asking, please, if he can come on the mission. Aron kneels down and places a gentle hand on his shoulder. "Not this time, Pawełek, but soon." He returns to standing, glances over at Shmuel, then at Róża.

"I will see you soon as I can, Różyczka," he says, and lopes out of the shop.

By the time Róża steps into the main square, Aron is nowhere in sight.

For the next two days, Róża listens as Chana bemoans her assignment—to stay and cook, per Sonia's orders, despite Chana's pleas to join the mission.

"I don't understand it. I would fight courageously."

"Yes, you would." Róża doesn't mention Chana's utter lack of training with a gun.

"I'm more fit than both Fregel sisters put together."

"But who would make soup for us, Chana? Would you leave us to subsist on their concoctions?" Secretly, or not so secretly, Róża is grateful that Chana wasn't permitted to go. She is grateful, too, for the protected sleeping bunk and the ready food here. She joins a small table of women at lunch.

After the others disperse, a young mother asks Róża to hold her baby, Issi, while she takes a bowl of soup.

Róża protests, but already he is placed in her arms. As he
wriggles against her, she feels a contracting in her uterus,
a tingling in her breasts. She is transported back to new
motherhood, to holding the warm bundle of her own baby
close, the mingling of calm and utter joy. A lullaby comes
to her lips, the beginning of a hen's *cucoo. No.*

This baby's heft, his doughy smell, his cry packed with
gaping need—it is all too much for Róża. She thrusts him
back into his mother's arms.

"I'm sorry, I can't help you."

"But, please—"

"I said I *can't.*"

Róża walks away, her body pulsing with ache, with sorrow. How can she possibly explain to this mother, whose
child is safe beside her? What is whole does not comprehend
what is torn until it, too, is in shreds.

Near dusk on the mission's third day, Róża trudges to the
watch post where she first encountered Hershel on patrol.
Little Paweł is there with him, keeping watch.

"Any word?"

"No," says Hershel.

"No," says Paweł.

A light snow dusts the air. Back near the campfire, the
falling flakes glint like fireflies.

Despite what she's been telling herself about Aron—that
she's only just met him; that she can't possibly grow at-
tached to another person she may yet lose; that she needs to
stay focused on her mission to find Shira—Róża has been
awaiting his return.

The following night, five of the seven fighters—Aron not
among them—stagger in, exhausted and bedraggled. Róża

sees who's there, who isn't. She doesn't wait to learn what's happened, doesn't ask for the story, the details; she runs, half-hunched, to the dugout, another burial, and curls in her bunk, knees pulled tight, her wet cheek pressed against the cold, damp earthen wall. What ruckus trails in from the crowd around the fire she blocks out by burying herself beneath straw, covering her eyes and ears with her arms slung over her face.

When she feels a hand on her shoulder, she shrugs it off, refusing to open her eyes. "Chana, no! Just leave me—"

The hand finds her cheek, and it smells of metal and smoke. Before Róża can sit up, Aron's hands are cradling her face. Instinctively, Róża wraps him in her arms, rough straw stuck between them.

"Why didn't you return with the others? I thought—"

"Itzhak hurt his ankle; I helped him back, slowly."

Aron leans in to kiss her, and Róża's insides go taut and fluttery, until unbidden thoughts wedge in: wild carrot seed; blood on snow.

He must feel her shudder because he shifts to her side, nuzzles his face in her hair.

"It's all right, Różyczka. We can just hold each other awhile."

A small cry escapes Róża's throat. She pushes her thoughts away and pulls Aron close.

Chapter 35

Before vespers, Zosia walks to Mother Agnieszka's spare chamber. Despite the fierce cold outside, she tugs at the window and opens it a crack, hoping that her bird will hear, that he will come with news of her mother. Hands healed, she cradles the violin in the crook of her arm and tunes it, her shallow breath slowing as she finds each note.

She practices Bloch's "Nigun," which Pan Skrzypczak taught her was the second of the three-part *Baal Shem*, composed in memory of Bloch's mother. She thinks of her own mother, wishing to be hopeful, yet the music's every note is infused with a haunting melancholy.

Zosia still remembers home, her family: that particular moment on Friday nights before everyone took their seats at the dinner table, lighted candles flickering in their eyes. There would be a hush and then they'd settle, and each would tell stories of their week, at the bakery, at university, in the workshop. As the war drew closer, the stories changed, grew darker; unasked questions sat on their lips and worry lodged in the lines of their faces. Still, they played their music afterward—folk songs, gypsy dances, the *insistence* of hope—escalating to a fever pitch, ending in meditation.

Zosia thinks she can hear those same songs alive inside the "Nigun"—until it plunges into discordance and darkness. The moan of chords, the bow pressed upon two strings at once, then the sound narrowing to a single note as the music slows and slips into echoes and finally cries out: a solitary wail, repeating, higher and softer, until it trails off, no longer heard.

Zosia lingers, bow on string even after the sound stops. Flecks of white rosin drift and float into the surrounding air. She is expected in the chapel soon. Still, she extends her packing ritual: loosening her bow and re-stowing the sponge and pad; laying the violin in the case; lowering its lid and snapping it shut. For an extra beat, she stands motionless and listens. In the ringing silence, she pulls the window closed and scurries out of the chamber, through the corridor, into the bruised night.

But Zosia doesn't make it to the chapel. A German soldier roaming the convent grounds has followed the sound of her playing and stops her now along the outside corridor.

"It was you playing the violin. Yes?"

The soldier's pale eyes glow yellow by the lantern. Zosia nods, too terrified to speak.

"Good. You will play a recital. Fetch your violin."

"Now?" Zosia wants to ask, but a nearby gunshot startles her into silence. If only she could summon help, but all the sisters are at vespers and the soldier stands blocking the pathway to the chapel.

Her legs quake as she retrieves her violin from Mother

Agnieszka's chamber, the soldier following close behind. They come to stand outside the chapel. Sister Nadzieja spots them through a transom window and whispers to Mother Agnieszka, who comes out.

"Good evening, Herr Mueller. May I ask what is happening?"

"A recital. My *Oberleutnant* will be arriving any minute—he enjoys music and this will be a special welcome for him."

Mother Agnieszka holds her eyes steady on Zosia as she speaks. "Very well. We'll assemble in the calefactory."

Whether vespers has ended or has been interrupted, Zosia doesn't know; all she knows is the calefactory is near instantly transformed into a recital hall, with once fine, now shabby armchairs reserved for the soldiers.

The nuns, their faces as white as the starched cloth at their cheeks, rush about, arranging the children in rows. The children squirm and fidget, excited at the night's unexpected turn. Zosia's belly jitters. Her hands seem hardly to belong to her—they shake so violently—and she can't think what to play. Definitely not "Nigun," though she just practiced it. Not Brahms's Scherzo either. She might break down in the middle of it. Sister Alicja quickly ties a kerchief around Zosia's head—"This will keep your hair out of your face"—before she lights additional lanterns at the front of the room.

The soldier leads in his comrades: one, towering in height and stone-faced, with fancy insignia on his collar and armband; the other, stocky and chuckling, in a plain brown uniform jacket, his hand on the pistol in its holster. As they enter, the room goes silent.

Zosia sends a pleading look to Mother Agnieszka, who bobs her head in a calming, rhythmic motion. Zosia struggles to breathe.

It occurs to Zosia to play the rhapsodic middle of Sarasate's *Zigeunerweisen*. She recently practiced it with Sister Nadzieja. Tuning her violin hastily, she quarter turns, hardly noticeable, to avoid directly facing the soldiers and the children seated behind them. She puts bow to string to start—her arm steady despite how nervous she feels inside—and plays, the guiding rhythm a Romani march, soft and introspective. In her mind, her bird, solitary, restless, seeks out a resting place in the icy branches of a tree. His warbling notes reverberate in the night sky like a call and response: *Are you there? Yes, I am here. Where? Right here. Settle yourself. Settle.*

A long, rising note, barely audible, ends the middle sections—a gloomy place to stop. Zosia takes a chance and continues, playing the final movement: upbeat and rousing, a showpiece. As she keeps watch on the intricate fingering and bowing, she really performs now, angling outward to the audience, aware of the sound echoing in the room, escalating, frenzied, and exciting. The last measures push Zosia, and she rises to their challenge with the quickest of strokes and wild plucking. She feels expansive as never before, legs rooted, bow-arm flying, her fingers dancing between the strings. She closes her eyes. The music soars beyond her own sensibilities, into the listening crowd. She finishes with a strong, dramatic bow stroke.

An uneasy silence follows. All eyes turn to the *Oberleutnant*. His previously severe expression has grown soft. When he speaks, it is as if regaining a lost voice.

"Amazing," he says in German.

Kasia begins applauding. The nuns join, and the children laugh and clap with a jubilance unknown in the convent's confines. The soldiers clap too. Zosia floods with relief. The only ones who sit unmoved are Ula and Adela.

Before tonight, Zosia only ever really wished to be heard by her bird, by her mother. As terrifying as it was, she loved performing for an audience.

When the men get up from their chairs, they are newly gracious. They leave without taking anything from the kitchen, without holding roll call.

Next morning, Zosia lifts her blanket to her face and breathes into it before making up her bed and wetting her hair in the bathroom sink. Sister Alicja came in the middle of the night to bleach it, and now Zosia hopes an extra rinse will take some of the smell out. With her head in the basin, she reaches for a towel, but Ula and Adela step in and block the shelf. Zosia retracts her arm and wrings out her hair by hand. She turns quickly to leave, but Ula gets in front of her.

"Your hair looks like straw."

Adela reaches out to touch it. "Why is it so stiff and wiry?"

Ula grabs a clump too. "And what kind of color is this?"

Both girls tug, hard, before letting go.

Ula and Adela walk out of the bathroom, toward the refectory. Hair dripping and in stocking feet, Zosia trails them as they slip into the larder. She waits a few seconds, then opens the door to catch them snatching rolls from the bread box.

"I will get you punished for this." Zosia's voice shakes, but she thrusts her face forward, not backing down.

"You wouldn't," Adela counters.

"You make any more trouble for me and I will summon Sister Alicja. You'll see, she will take my word over yours."

Ula and Adela stare in surprise. Zosia takes a slight step toward them, daring only because of what's at stake.

A moment passes. Ula places her roll back in the bread box and brushes flour from her whitened fingertips. Adela bites into her roll, then stuffs it into her pocket as she walks past Zosia, out of the refectory, Ula rushing after her.

Chapter 36

Aron seeks out Róża in the nighttime, just to talk, to hold her in sleep. Nestled close in her bunk, he asks her, "What happened to your family?" And so she tells him how the soldiers came to her parents' house in Gracja.

"At first, it was to ransack my father's luthier workshop. They smashed his workbenches, stole his tools. Spilled his varnishes everywhere and even broke one of his violins. A few weeks later, they came for us."

She tells him how her parents hid her in their closet; how she reached for the frosting tip in the pocket of her mother's coat while she blocked out the awful thumping sounds, her parents stumbling down the stairs.

But she cannot manage to tell him that she'd lost Natan, shot in a trench he'd been forced to dig, and that Shira was *with* her there in the closet, hunched amid wool blazers and camel-hair overcoats—yet is not with her still.

The words Róża swallows while awake script her dreams while she sleeps.

She is crocheting tiny bird scarves for the coming winter. Her fingers work the yarn quickly, three neat stitches across

*and one stitch down, over and over again. But it's not yarn
at all, it is copper-wrapped gut spooling from the pocket
of a splayed-open violin case, and each tug tightens the
wire's grip on the small bird tangled within it. Three across,
one down; three across, one down. Róża stitches on, until
she hears a frantic flapping, a strangled chirp.*

"*Nie!*"

"You had another nightmare." Aron leans over her, troubled.

Róża tries to shake it off. Her hands throb. Splotches bloom
red on her skin, as if pecked. Did she harm herself in sleep?
Róża turns toward the earthen wall. She tucks her hands
gingerly beneath the backs of her thighs so Aron won't see.

For weeks, they sleep entwined, Róża's head pressed against
Aron's shoulder, his arm wrapped around her hip. Until the
night, when time both stops and pulses, when Róża sets herself free to feel and to remember—then all that has been ex-
iled rises up and it is her first night with Natan, his soft lips
on hers and her body opening to the sweet, sharp wholeness
that brought her unknown pleasure, unimaginable hope.
And it is night after night with Henryk—his eyes, then his
heavy frame atop hers, Róża praying that Shira would remain asleep. And it is the night when Shira was taken. *Gone.*
The feel of her padded hands and the smoothness of her
belly, the smell of her hair, her wide-open curious stare. As
Aron moves gently inside her, Róża buries her face in his
chest. He wraps his arms tight around her.

As Róża pairs with Aron, Chana pairs with Hershel. Hershel
cooks alongside Chana on her shifts and Chana accompanies
Hershel on his walk each day to the patrol station.

Róża is surprised to see Chana holding a gun one morning.

"Yes, I am learning to shoot. Hershel is teaching me. Stop looking at me like that."

Róża is repairing torn jackets late one afternoon when Hershel rushes by, shouting, "German soldiers! They are coming!"

In a matter of seconds everyone is running, some to the bunks, others to the steepest area of the forest. Questions fly from every direction.

"How close?"

"How many?"

"Where will we go?"

Aron comes in for Róża. "Cross the stream and take the steep pass with the others. The Germans won't follow there; they don't know the terrain. Go as quickly as you can, then wait. I'll come when—"

"Aron, please, come with me *now*; I can't—"

"I have to stay and fight. I'll follow, I promise you."

Chana runs past with two rifles. Róża catches her by the arm. "Chana, where are you going? We have to run, right away."

"I'm fighting."

"No! You can't!"

But there is no time to argue. They both hear the rumble of gunfire. Chana dives into the metal shop for bullets. Róża runs, as Aron instructed her, toward the stream.

Sonia is at the water's edge, directing people to cross it. They hesitate before stepping into the icy flow. "Go on!" she yells. Róża wades in, submerging the boots Aron gave her. They soak in seconds. She instinctively jolts back, hardly able to catch her breath, but then she pushes forward, the cold water seeping through her pants, searing her calves, her thighs. It's a struggle to make headway; the water is deep and the rocks slippery. But eventually she reaches the other side and follows the trail of people, dripping and shivering, down the pass.

Some who crossed ahead carried their saws and other tools. Already they've built a fire and are at work on temporary shelters. Others grabbed sacks of potatoes and soup pots. They've been run out of camps before. Róża steps close to the fire, desperate to get dry and warm, then sets herself to starting a soup. Every few minutes she scans the top of the pass for Aron, for Chana.

Why don't they come already? The fire has not fully dried her clothing, and her boots are miserably wet still. With every crack of gunfire, Róża feels more despair.

At dusk Hershel stumbles down the pass.

"There were eight and we routed them," he says in heaving breaths. Someone helps peel off his soaking coat; someone else hands him a dry one. In the meantime people shout out names with the hope that he will report, "They're fine; they're on the way here now."

Róża stands, silent.

Hershel continues to gasp for air. His head is still in the skirmish. "They won't follow us down here. They don't know the deep woods like we do."

Sonia cuts in, "Nevertheless, we'll need to set up new patrols immediately."

A debate ensues about the best lookout spots.

Hershel says that a peasant, from whom they stole food and tools, scouted out their camp and told the Germans. "He led them to us; I saw."

Róża feels as though she may go crazy. It is near dark and no sign of others coming down.

"Hershel, please tell us," she finally begs. "Where are the others? Who didn't make it?"

Hershel looks up at Róża. The others go silent.

"Ilan and Mayer, may they rest in peace."

Sorrow mixes with relief as Róża thanks God that Aron and Chana are alive.

"Also we lost little Paweł," Hershel says in a breaking voice. "They're burying him now. Ruthie couldn't corral him and he got hit."

Paweł: partisan-in-miniature; Issi's older brother; he asked Aron practically once a day when he'd be old enough to go on his first mission. Róża kept her distance from the children here, except for *him*.

Róża looks around at the other mothers, enveloping their children. Ruthie—whom she'd refused to help by holding Issi—bent over the hillside, her hands clutching dirt.

Something breaks loose inside Róża and skitters down the stairs of her heart. Her fingers feel for the stitches at the waistband of her pants, the re-stowed address card. She can't wait any longer; she must get to Shira *now*.

She builds the case in her mind: She knows how to survive in the woods on her own. And once she has Shira with her she can determine where to go next, whether to return here or find another place to hide. She wishes she could see with her own eyes Aron and Chana safe after the attack; but she doesn't wait. Her clothes and boots well-enough dried, she turns from the fire, stuffs her pockets with potatoes, and begins walking, away from the newly forming camp, in search of Celestyn and the convent that's held Shira in safekeeping.

Chapter 37

Spring 1944

The *Oberleutnant* returns to the convent and demands another recital. It is early evening. Mother Agnieszka intercepts Zosia, carrying clean towels from the laundry, to retrieve her violin, quick. As Zosia walks nervously to the calefactory, her fears focus on Adela being in the audience. *What might she say or do?*

But the *Oberleutnant* is there alone. Settled in an armchair, he speaks kindly to Zosia, encouraging her to take her time with the tuning and warm-up. Mother Agnieszka stands in the corner, her hands clamped tightly in front of her habit.

Zosia takes a preparatory breath, a deep, silent inhale and exhale. Pan Skrzypczak taught her this, though she'd already learned such controlled breathing in the barn with her mother. She plays the second part of Bruch's Violin Concerto no. 1, lyrical and languorous. Though she is nervous, her playing is smooth. Pan Skrzypczak told Zosia that Joachim advised Bruch on this work and that he not only received its dedication but was the soloist to first perform it. Zosia likes to think of this: another bit of music that kept Joachim from loneliness.

The movement builds with sentiment and passion, then subsides to a tranquil close. When Zosia brings the violin to rest beneath her arm, the *Oberleutnant*, flush cheeked, applauds. "Max Bruch?"

"Yes."

"Do you know that his wife inscribed on his tombstone, 'Music is the language of God'?"

Zosia didn't know this. She doesn't dare answer.

The *Oberleutnant* stands. From his coat pocket he produces a waxy bag with a jam-filled roll inside, which he hands to Zosia.

Zosia looks at it, stunned. It smells as if it were just baked, with powdered sugar sprinkled on top. There has been so little food at mealtimes, her stomach nearly leaps to her mouth. It takes her a moment to find her voice. "Thank you."

"Thank *you*," the *Oberleutnant* says. "I will come again." And with a nod to Mother Agnieszka, he departs.

Zosia looks to Mother Agnieszka for permission to eat the roll.

Its taste is like a cloud, airy and sweet, with a tang of plum jam so perfect as to mix earth with heaven. The last bite is practically in her mouth when she holds back, saving a taste for Kasia, a taste for her mother.

Mother Agnieszka interrupts Zosia's next violin lesson to confer with Pan Skrzypczak. How much music has Zosia mastered? How quickly can she learn more, if the *Oberleutnant* keeps asking to hear her play? Mother Agnieszka's face is pinched with distress, but Zosia is pleased because

Pan Skrzypczak agrees to give her an extra lesson every week.

Sister Alicja ushers Zosia to the side chapel for a class on receiving communion. "Because you're seven," she says, and Zosia thinks of past birthday parties, hers and her mother's, with music and frosted cake and treasure hunts along the river. Birthdays in the orphanage are marked with thin slices of spice bread after lunch.

The chapel hovers cavernous and gloomy, its dark cross-beams stark against the white walls. Almost no light enters from the small stained-glass windows that dot the wall just below the pitched ceiling.

Other girls troop in and Zosia hears one of them whisper, "We are meant to consume the blood and body of Christ."

"What?"

"That's right." She points to the wine chalice and wafer cup on the altar. "The wine and wafer are blood and bone."

Zosia grows dizzy, fearing she might vomit. Sister Alicja kneels beside her. She puts a finger upon Zosia's cheek, gently, like the flutter of wings.

"You needn't worry, Zosia. It is a holy sacrament. And it is accompanied by a beautiful chant. Let me teach that to you now."

Sister Alicja sings it and almost immediately it is conjoined in Zosia's mind with companion notes, minor in key, that deepen and enrich it. Zosia is calmed, less fearful of her communion, and eager to get to her violin later and play what she hears inside.

As the day approaches, Zosia and the other girls excitedly try on lacy white dresses and shiny white shoes, stored in the chapel closet, pulled out each spring. Kasia offers to braid Zosia's hair—"It will look pretty for your service!"—but Zosia refuses. Kasia is trying to cheer her, Zosia knows, as when she invited her to join in on the prank of putting potato skins upon the mouths of the portraits. But Zosia worries. Supplies have grown scarcer and Sister Alicja has had to stretch out the bleachings of her hair. She doesn't want Kasia to spot brown at the roots. And if she offers to weave a daisy crown?

Zosia takes to wearing a white kerchief over her head daily, tied with the tiniest knot at the back. She studies hard for her communion. "Communion" is not a word she understands, though she thinks it might mean *connection*, and she feels she should want connection with Jesus, who the nuns say is the greatest teacher of all. Safe within the parables, prayers, and hymns—nowhere a spark for others' hatred of her; nowhere the danger of losing all she might come to love—she finds her devotion to Him.

When her name—Zosia Nowakówna—is called, no other name stirs within her, even as the air's grassy scent evokes hay, nights entwined with her mother. She solemnly walks forward and kneels, opening her mouth to receive the sacrament, dry and papery. Afterward, she sings and prays. The littlest children think she is trying to be a nun.

Chapter 38

Róża was emboldened when she left the camp, but now, in the woods without company or protection, knowing that Germans could be nearby, she struggles to keep her doubts in check. *What if I am caught? What will become of Shira then?* Several times she comes close to back-tracking, but she propels onward: she must see that Shira is all right.

For days, it pours. Her boots soak again; her feet chill, then chafe. The wetness seeps to her bones. She sleeps in burrows of sticky mud and damp pine needles. When she walks, she varies her steps, aiming always for the cover of leaves rather than the earthen ground that sucks at her soles and imprints deep tracks. She prays that Natan's compass has her properly directed due south.

Her last substantial meal was the soup she made at the new campsite. Since then, she's rationed the five potatoes she stuffed into her pockets before leaving—too few, yet more than she was entitled to take for herself.

She has one potato left.

* * *

Zosia is folding cloth napkins at the long refectory table—
though there is hardly any food, only thistle soup and groats
and dusty bread—when Sister Nadzieja rushes in. She is
dressed to travel and she is holding Zosia's coat and hat.

"Come, Zosia. You must get into the carriage right away."

"Where are we going?" Zosia had been in her private musical world, chaotic compositions of raw yearning, unlike the
orderly music of the church, filling her ears, her head. Only
now does she register what's happening around her: people
running in the street, sirens wailing closer than ever. The
smell of burning.

"We have to get out of the city. They are bombing everything."

"No. I can't!" Her yellow bird was to bring her mother
here. If Zosia leaves, her mother won't be able to find her.

Sister Nadzieja wrestles to get Zosia into her coat, but
Zosia twists away, her arms flapping.

"You must, we all must. I'll keep you safe, I promise—no
one will spot you in the carriage."

"But this is where she'll come for me!"

"Zosia, I'll carry you if I have to. I have your blanket
and your violin packed. And your outdoor shoes are here.
Quick, put them on."

"You don't understand, my mama—"

Zosia cries bitterly as she is lifted into the carriage, its
benches near filled with girls from the younger children's
room. *Please, I don't want to go!* As the carriage jerks around
the corner and Siostry Felicjanki disappears, she feels an
imaginary chain snap inside her.

* * *

The streets overflow with people fleeing the city. Zosia stares at the children perched on their fathers' shoulders, cradled in their mothers' arms, propped on backs, dragged along sideways. All around, terrified people rush past, layered in extra clothes, bowed under the weight of suitcases, bags, and bundles. One lady, her arms stretched to their full length to convey a painting, trips over the broken sidewalk. Zosia sputters and coughs, then goes silent.

The air is clotted with smoke and dust. On bombed-out city blocks, the overpowering smell of sulfur joins the scents of yeast sours and rye as they pass the remnants of a bakery; singed flesh and rot as they pass a gutted butcher shop; burnt hide and cedar oil as they pass a tannery in ruins. Zosia limits her closemouthed breaths until, as they begin to head into the countryside, the scents of unburnt moss and pine signal fresher air.

It takes hours to reach the new convent—a strange compound of buildings, dark and cold, connected by a confounding maze of corridors, far away from ul. Poniatowskiego 33. Zosia isn't cheered by the grand pipe organ in the chapel or by the spacious girls' room, a common room transformed. She grows frantic for Kasia. Every few minutes, she erupts into sobs.

"Where is Kasia? Why isn't she here yet?" she demands.

Sister Nadzieja assures Zosia that she is on the way.

"And Sister Alicja and Mother Agnieszka?"

"They will also be arriving shortly."

They come in the next carriage—Sister Alicja embraces her in a warm hug and Kasia hitches to her, not letting go— yet Zosia remains distraught. By nightfall, she is joined in her sobbing as word arrives that six boys and the two sisters charged to evacuate them were caught in the bombings. One of those sisters, the resident baker, Halina, was beloved by the children because she was always willing to play chasing games in the late afternoons. But Zosia liked her for different reasons: because one of the cats resembled her and because she smelled of bread, like Zosia's grandmother.

Amid the keening and chaos, some of the children wander the halls, exploring, but Zosia does not want to see any more of this place. It smells musty, and the stone statues, everywhere, have scary, vacant eyes.

Sister Nadzieja checks on Zosia as she squats in a dark corner, squeezing her eyes shut, rocking forward and back.

"Zosia—"

"When will Pan Skrzypczak come?"

"I don't know."

Zosia hears despondency in Sister Nadzieja's voice.

"He was going to teach me new music—"

Zosia develops a fever. She lies, red cheeked and shivering, in a bed that's been jammed in a narrow hallway, away from the other girls. Her hair is slick; her eyelids flutter open and closed. The unfamiliar surroundings disorient her further.

Sometimes she recognizes the people who tend to her: Sister Alicja laying a cool compress on her forehead; Mother Agnieszka carrying a fresh blanket to her bed. Other times, she doesn't know who these robed people are. They keep calling her Zosia, but she is not: she is *Shira*! She lives in the barn with her mother, and before that she was in her grandparents' house. Her *tata* was there, too, with his watery voice and tickly beard.

She wants her snuggle blanket, the one with the bumpy

edging. She tries to yank off her covers, but they are heavy and taut. She kicks and flails, she throws her pillow. She dreams.

She is with her mother in the barn, but her bird is missing; she can't find him anywhere. She searches the hay, frantic. "Mama, please, will you look for him?" and she watches, satisfied, as her mother leaves for the farmhouse. But her bird is there, perched in the rafters. He is cloaked entirely in black like a nun. His wet-black eyes, usually so bright against his yellow face, now look muted and flat. In his beak are crushed white flower petals.

"Mama!" Zosia yells, and flings her arms out to her sides to steady herself. She has to clutch the rails of her bed to keep from tipping out.

"Easy now, we're just moving your bed again. Your fever has you yelling out names."

"Names? Where am I?"

Zosia's bed is now in the nuns' corridor. Sister Alicja is beside her, prayer beads in her lap, a hand on Zosia's forehead.

Zosia wakes next with long-ago music in her head: a sleep song, a hen's call, her mother's gentle voice.

Mama? she asks.

But it is not her mother who touches her cheek, who takes her hand, who nurses her back to wellness.

She was with her parents in her dreams.

Sister Alicja told her that when she was sick, she called out names.

Her mother's? Her father's?

Maryla taught her made-up new names for them, but she only ever knew them as *Mama*, as *Tata*.

Did she yell out her *own* given name? This thought, too, brings a rising shame, as her hiding name has taken hold deeply within her. For so long she's thought of herself *not* as Shira but as Zosia. She took her communion with it.

Zosia worries about what she's blurted out, and she worries about what she's left behind and forgotten. As much as possible, she keeps her mouth shut, her violin her only mouthpiece, her spoken words coming out in half-swallowed, halted bursts.

Chapter 39

Róża reaches Celestyn's outskirts after weeks of walking through thicketed pastures, thistles biting at her ankles, her empty canteen bobbing against her chest. Dried mud cakes to her skin; her scalp crawls once again with lice. Spotting a puddle, she bends to it, bringing a handful of brown water to her lips. It tastes of ash.

Everywhere, there is smoke. Throughout the city, buildings have been bombed away, and some are still burning. But nowhere are there signs of German soldiers, German cars.

She darts down an abandoned street, head lowered, taking note of where the sewers are—she'll drop into one if she has to. Even if she can't retrieve Shira right away, she is determined to find the convent. And if, as it appears, the German army has in fact retreated, maybe it will be safe enough—maybe she needn't wait much longer—to see her girl.

Róża takes cover in an alleyway behind a row of outsize refuse cans until nightfall. She wants to rummage through the cans—for food, for newspapers—but she doesn't dare.

She remains hunched and solitary in the dusky shadows. Once it is completely dark, Róża traverses the long city blocks, one bloody, blistered foot in front of the other. She skirts mounds of crumbled brick, shattered stucco roof tiles. She does not pass another soul.

Is the city under curfew? What if someone is watching from a window this very moment?

Even if the Germans are gone, she may be the target of certain Poles.

She keeps to the shadows, moving quickly, scanning for street names. In her head she recites the convent address story—thirty-three-year-old Józef crosses the long bridge, looking toward the heavens—over and over. There are church spires everywhere, and Róża fears she is turning circles as she skitters first in one direction, then in another, toward them. But then she catches sight of a sign indicating the way to Siostry Felicjanki.

She stops. She has made it!

A melody, bright and exultant, comes to her, reminding her of Shira. She takes the melody up, lets it repeat in her mind.

Before rounding the street corner, Róża allows herself to imagine, in a way she hasn't dared until this moment, Shira and her together again. Safe. In a tucked-away cabin somewhere, eating soup with kreplach and sweet lokshen kugel. Shira chattering away, little hands cupped around her imaginary, still alive bird, who chirps aloud his melodious eighteen-note song. Bathed clean, hair washed and braided, maybe tied off with daisies, a pretty frosted cake for dessert.

Smoke billows scarf-like behind the street sign, luminous in the moonlight. Róża's hands rise to her dirt-stained cheeks, her protruding cheekbones. She wonders if Shira will recognize her. After staring at the sign a minute longer, Róża takes a deep breath and turns onto ul. Poniatowskiego.

Where every minute of every day she has envisioned a tall gate, an arched doorway, a sturdy stone church sheltering her child, Róża finds mounds of brick and rubble. The only thing she recognizes here is a twisted lamppost. Her hands wrap around it as her stomach heaves and her knees buckle beneath her.

How could this be?

Róża has the overwhelming urge to lie down, her body a deserted crossroads. She'd survived—she'd even found friendship and love—while Shira was here in this bomb zone. Why hadn't she thought to come for her right away, as soon as she saw that children could live in the family camp? Why had she ever waited?

Her rapturous melody morphs into a monstrous atonal accusation, punctuating her shame. A dizzying series of crescendos—the scream of shells, the collapse of buildings all around—ends with a falling chord that searches, desperate, for the music that will complete it. It finds none.

Róża feels around in her pocket for the cyanide pill.

At bedtime, Zosia cannot find her shred of blanket. She looks beneath her mattress, in her dresser, even in the secret drawer Sister Alicja recently allotted her for saving bits of food for her mother. *How can it have disappeared like this?* She looks again under her pillow and between the sheets at the foot of the bed, beginning to feel panicked. *Did Adela or Ula dare to take it?* They haven't caused her trouble since before moving convents, since she caught them raiding the larder. Eventually Zosia notices that her sheets are freshly laundered. Maybe her blanket got taken up with the afternoon wash?

She rushes through the corridors where the statues and dark portraits are still strange to her. She stops just short of the washing room, humid and slick and soapy, when she spots Sister Olga and Mother Agnieszka.

Neither would approve of her late night errand, so she conceals herself behind the open washroom door and strains to listen as Mother Agnieszka tasks Sister Olga with various arrangements for next Sunday's service. A guest organist will be coming for the feast day, she is saying. Zosia's mind runs to the propers of the liturgy until a sharpness in Mother Agnieszka's tone brings Zosia back to her errand and to fragments of their conversation.

"What are you holding in your hands? Sister Olga, is that Zosia's blanket?"

"Yes, and I want to show . . . omething odd at the seam. These stitches—"

"Never you mind about a little girl's . . . I'm here to talk with you about . . . for Sunday."

"But—"

Zosia's fingers float to the kerchief knot at the nape of her neck and she remembers: her mother sewed in the same rhythm she braided: long threaded strokes punctuated by a gentle tug.

"Sister Olga, I understand . . . don't like to launder the children's personal . . . If a child's security blanket got caught up with the sheets . . . mistake. I'll take it now."

"But what if . . . a *code*?" Zosia hears something unexpected in Sister Olga's voice: a tinge of fear. "Do you think . . . haps show the commandant?"

"Absolutely not! Now I insist . . . back to folding laundry.

The light down here is . . . and your imagination . . . wild to-night."

At Zosia's communion ceremony, Sister Olga had mut-tered something about shoddy baptism records. Zosia had stopped midstride—what baptism records?—but Mother Agnieszka nodded her forward and she'd marched up the aisle in her pretty white dress.

Zosia rushes back through the corridor and climbs into bed, her breath unsteady. Tears come now, not only be-cause Sister Olga may have discovered what her mother took pains to hide but because no matter how she tries, she can't fully recall her mother's face. The features come to her disjointed and shifting, as if viewed through an ever-turning kaleidoscope—her soft, worried eyes the color of midnight; the hollow dip just below her collarbone; the small mole marking the rim of her cheek—yet Zosia can't put the pieces together in her mind, can't remember *her mother*.

What she *can* vividly remember is hiding—burying her-self beneath hay. Pursing her mouth tight and inhaling soundlessly through her nose. Suppressing a swallow, stifling a sneeze. Ignoring an itch, a cramp. Constricting her bow-els. Not seeing into the far or even the middle distance, but staring at the hay and boards inches from her eyes. What she can vividly remember is how her mother pleaded with her, needed her, to disappear.

Zosia positions herself in the bed so as to hold completely still through the night. The start position makes all the dif-ference: shoulders and head lined up straight, never tilted to one side, never crook'd in an arm.

She wakes with a start as dawn's light filters through the high window. Her blanket is back on her pillow. She thinks of stowing it beneath her mattress or under the blouses in her bureau. But then she thinks of Olga searching the children's room.

She remembers how, when soldiers first came to Gracja, her grandmother buried silver candlesticks and precious photographs in coffee tins in their garden. Zosia slips out of bed and, as quietly as she can, patters to the storage shed. She takes a small spade and at the edge of the courtyard, beneath a privet, she digs a hole. Before lowering her blanket into it, she inhales the must that lingers beneath its soapy scent and runs a finger over its edge, over and across and over again, tracing the distinctive bulges that spell out her history: her mother's stitches, the braille of her childhood. The air is damp and chilly. Zosia covers her blanket over with soil. She sets down a flat rock, a single daisy on top of it. For the rest of the day, her fingers hold the scent of wet earth.

Chapter 40

Get up, quickly! You passed out." A woman's voice, a hiss.

Róża squints against the morning sky, the acrid stench of her own vomit.

She feels rough hands upon her, someone attempting to drag her from the rubble. Her body aches. Slowly she turns her neck. A white-haired woman with eyes like the sea grips Róża's shoulders and tugs; then she scurries around to clasp her ankles. Róża is leaden.

"You'll be killed!" The woman yanking at her is old and blocky and strong.

"Just leave me be."

"There are soldiers still about, I tell you. If someone sees you—"

Róża's eyes roam the rubble in the burnt orange of dawn. Why is this woman trying to help her? She doesn't want to get up. She wants to close her eyes.

"Pani Byczek will be the first to summon them. She's always patrolling for transgressors. You must come with me!"

Róża is too depleted to fight this Good Samaritan, whatever her motive. She clambers to standing and lets herself be pulled, tripping over broken brick and stone, as the lady shepherds her down the block and around the corner.

"In here." The lady presses her into what looks like a locksmith's shop, cool and dim and smelling of shaved metal. Past a long counter covered in key molds and gauges and pins, a single bulb casts a circle of light upon a table. The lady motions to a chair and Róża drops into it, her raw, ripped feet aching.

The lady disappears, and when she returns with a bowl of watery soup, Róża nearly spills it down her chin in her eagerness to eat it. It tastes like a garden, the rooted earth.

"When was the city bombed?" Róża's voice is as shaky as the spoon in her hand.

"About two weeks ago."

"Is it possible that anyone from the orphanage survived?" The cyanide pill waits in her pocket.

"I don't know."

A sudden, darting rage: Maryla should never have brought Shira here. The nuns should never have taken her in. It wasn't safe! How could they have agreed to hide her here, when it wasn't safe?

Shame rears up inside her again. It is her *own* fault. She should never have let Shira go in the first place. She labors to breathe.

"Where are you from?"

Róża doesn't answer.

"Do you realize there are people here who would shoot a Jew on sight?"

She knows. So why didn't she let me die on the broken stone? Róża doesn't say anything.

The lady sighs and takes hold of Róża's trembling arm.

"You can't be out in daylight, that much is for certain. Why don't you lie down for a bit?" She leads Róża to a mattress tucked in the corner, draped by blankets.

As soon as Róża lies down, she falls precipitously to sleep. But minutes later, she wakes, panting for air, blinking away images of ruffled feathers, cupped hands.

The lady is sitting in a tattered chair nearby. "I'll make you some hot water while you rest."

But Róża won't rest now. She stares down at her own hands. They are dusted white from the convent rubble.

Part 3

The mother, too, hears music in her head. The melody is discordant and accusatory. When she covers her ears with her hands, a different tune—a lullaby—asserts itself, more painful for its sweet, rocking lyricism.

The lullaby tells of a hen who sets out for a glass of tea to bring home to her waiting chicks. It is the girl's favorite, and it is accompanied by the lilt of a kept promise:

The hen returns.

Chapter 41

Summer 1944

The Samaritan's name is Lidia, and she is one of a small network of Celestyn women who, under cover of darkness, shuttle Róża to safe cellars and attics and any number of abandoned buildings with locks that are broken or can be picked. Each presses bread into Róża's hands and conveys the latest news: Minsk has been liberated; the Soviets have taken Vilna. But none knows whether any orphans survived the bombings at ul. Poniatowskiego 33. At the time, everyone was hunkered in shelters amid the rain of wall plaster and the cartwheels of ceiling fragments, emerging afterward to find the entire city block destroyed.

Róża wakes each morning, herself in ruins. Lidia fetches her, forces a bowl of thin broth upon her, and occupies her with work assignments in the locksmith shop until another day passes.

Róża is half-grateful. She has no interest in befriending Lidia, who is both odd and intrusive in addition to generous; whose surveillance and taskmastering keeps Róża from acting on her impulse to step out of the shop, wander the open streets, wind up shot.

They copy keys for the safe houses in the area. Lidia's only outside contact with the operation is a puffy-faced man named Aleksy who delivers boxes of spare lock parts with keys concealed in false bottoms and retrieves them days later, all keys in duplicate, once again hidden.

Róża is a quick learner. She masters the key cutter and works with thick filing sticks to create the copies. Dust shavings float in the air. Her fingers stain dark gray, and she tastes iron on her lips day and night.

Several weeks pass in this way. Lidia fetches Róża before morning's light and escorts her out beneath evening's darkness. Best not to stay too long in any one place.

With the constant work comes an inkling of purpose: a rhythm in her hands as she and Lidia methodically cut and file the keys, then stow them away; a thump in her chest as Aleksy leaves the shop with another box wedged in the crook of his arm. One afternoon Róża points to a pile of spare blankets in the corner and says, "If I sleep here, we can work at night also." Lidia nods, her pale eyes shining.

Their resistance efforts—and the hot iron Lidia occasionally uses to smooth jagged bits of metal—prompt Róża to think of Chana. Chana told Róża how she once used her mother's clothes iron to finish a crème brûlée (incidentally, her most delicious egg dish), unleashing the fury of her mother *and* Miri—who had a date with Ari Bauer that night and had planned to press and then wear her nicest pleated skirt. Chana insisted the sugar would burn off and the iron would be good as new, but it was wrecked, repurposed for caramelizing projects only.

As she remembers it, a tightness rises from the pit of Róża's stomach and catches in her throat as the image of

Miri, splayed on the forest floor, calls up the stubborn flare of refusal to accept Shira's death.

So long as she hasn't *seen* her girl's body amid the rubble, can't she cling to the possibility that Shira is still alive?

Late summer, Russian tanks roll into Celestyn, signaling the liberation of the city. Lidia peels back a corner of the shop's black window covering to see the streets fill with people, shouting and hugging, kissing and crying. Bells from every church in the city begin tolling and toll on and on without ceasing.

Róża ventures out, apprehensively, her Semitic looks exposed in broad daylight. She can't find her footing amid the chaos and ruin, the jostling of people who stare at her and step widely out of her path as she passes. Her whole body quakes as she walks, as she poses questions on her lips. She is determined to find out what she can about the orphans of Siostry Felicjanki.

Some call Róża "kike" and stiffen and bristle around Lidia, turning heel in scorn. Yet one kindly woman who refused to evacuate a flat near ul. Poniatowskiego tells Róża of carriages circling the convent gate hours before the bombings. Another reports a nun leading a line of small girls along the cobbles. Róża pulls the photo fold from her pocket, torn and water damaged. "Please. Do you remember seeing *her* among them?" She points, with a shaking hand, to the faded photograph of Shira.

"I'm sorry, I don't know."

Róża goes from ministry to ministry, inquiring about the possibility of a Jewish girl hidden within the Felicjan orphanage. She meets with pitying looks and discomfited head shakes, but no useful information. Eventually she returns to the ruined convent area, mounds of rubble streaked pink by the dusk sky.

More than anything, she hopes to find someone who will tell her that the convent was evacuated, that the orphans were moved to safety before the bombings. Instead she meets a woman who witnessed two nuns and their wards caught in the destruction.

"I saw it with my own eyes. Those poor little children. The nuns too. Bless their souls."

The lady crosses herself. Róża squeezes her eyes shut.

"Are you certain?"

"Yes."

"Do you think it's possible that any of them survived?"

The woman describes what she saw. A little boy's body lying among the rubble. A nun's veil billowing in the dust. Róża can't accept it. Carriages were circling, and there were girls out near ul. Felicjanek. Perhaps Shira was injured, not dead. Róża sets out for the local hospital ward—corridors lined with limp, lopsided people, blinking up at the wavering lights—but does not find her there.

A Registry of Jewish Survivors opens in Celestyn. Róża pores over lists and sublists. Lidia accompanies her despite mounting pressure from neighbors—many of whom had appropriated apartments, furniture, and valuables left behind when people were taken—to stop helping "the Jew."

There is no single compilation of names, so they have to search each list separately. There are stacks of them. They sit at a small table, piled high with papers. Names that bear any resemblance—the given names Shipra, Shir, Shiraz, Shirel, Shirli; the surnames Choda, Chodorkow, Chodorowski—

drive Róża to despair. They are never paired up right, and the ages are way off, and she wonders: Did the sisters of the convent ever learn Shira's real name?

"It's no use. We'll never find her this way."

"You're certain you don't know the name they gave her?" Lidia asks.

"No." She takes the bent, mud-stained card out of her pocket. "This was supposed to be enough."

Róża can feel her face grow hot. She grips the table to steady herself. How could she have been so thoughtless, so stupid, as to not ask Shira's assigned Christian name before letting her go? Róża buries her face in her hands.

Upon returning to the locksmith shop, they find shattered windows, the floor stippled with glass.

Róża hastens to pick up the shards. "I need to leave you. You're not safe with me here."

Head bowed, Lidia reaches for a broom.

When Russian soldiers sweep through the convent, Mother Agnieszka closes the children into the kitchen. Adela boldly pokes a finger into a bin of flour and tastes it, puckering her lips. Mother Agnieszka does not chide her. She doesn't seem to notice the children at all. Her head is cocked toward the high window, her face alive with tremors as she listens for the sisters, scuttling through the halls, shutting themselves into their rooms.

Zosia hears the pounding of boots along the back corridor as soldiers move through the nuns' quarters; the yank of a bedroom door; a sister's high-pitched cry. Zosia steps nearer to Mother Agnieszka, but she's in her own shivery trance, fingers circling rosary beads, lips muttering silent prayers.

Eventually Sister Alicja arrives. She is the palest Zosia has ever seen, her habit in disarray, and her hair—which Zosia has *never* seen, the color of honey—pokes out sloppily from her headdress. She huddles with Mother Agnieszka, staring toward the courtyard with unfocused eyes.

Zosia thinks of her mother lying flat in the center of the loft, lost to the crossbeams and rafters. Henryk hustling down the ladder and out of the barn. Her bird burying low in her cupped hands. She floods with confusion. From overhearing the sisters' whispers all these past months, Zosia thought that the arrival of Russian soldiers would mean the end of the war. The chance to find her mother.

"Is the war over?" she asks.

Neither answers, so Zosia continues.

"Can we go back to *our* convent? Is it safe now, Sister Alicja?" If only they could return to their convent, she might be reunited with her mother, with Pan Skrzypczak.

Sister Alicja turns to Zosia, her expression dark. "No, Zosia, I'm afraid it is not at all safe."

Chapter 42

Róża squats in an abandoned apartment house across the street from where Siostry Felicjanki is supposed to be. Lidia thought it safest for her to leave Celestyn altogether, but she feels tethered to this place.

Twilight bathes the sidewalk. A warbler flits about in the dust. Róża stares out at the rubble and lets herself imagine: Shira has only just been *hiding* in the mounds of broken brick and stone. She is not buried by it but is sitting atop it in a pale frock, tricking everyone by her statuesque stillness and silence.

The next breezy day brings a new fantasy: Shira hopping across, her blanket billowing from her hand. Rain breaks the spell altogether, as it causes the rubble to turn gray and lose its powdery cover. Róża is unwilling to imagine Shira's skin as a match for that stone. She halts her vigil and heads for the streets.

Liberated Celestyn is lawless and chaotic and still dangerous for Jews. Róża moves through the streets quickly, eyes averted. Lidia insists on buying her food at the grocer's. But Róża scours the debris-filled alleys to find "Shira things"—

nubby pencils, an ink pen, stray papers, a child's book, soaked, all of its pages curled. To hold even a frayed bit of string gives her strength when she returns to check the survivors' registry, hoping, praying, that someone from the convent has submitted Shira's information using her proper name.

She steals glances at the children on the streets. She watches a baby in a pram, a toddler clasping her mother's skirt, teetering toward a park bench. The resemblances to Shira transcend all logic—this would be the season of Shira's eighth birthday—yet Róża continues as the resonances accrue in her mind and, collage-like, Shira rises up before her. Almond eyes, a heart-shaped face, a thick brown braid. It is for *this* that she walks on, block after block. Róża's heartbeat quickens, a wild happiness builds. Until, without warning, like a balloon overfilled, her hope bursts.

Róża closes herself back into her squat. She tells herself it's best to lie down, to breathe deeply, to try to relax. But rather than relaxing, she is beset by another vision—a memory of her first night in the woods.

She is in her forest dugout, feeling not so much bereft of Shira as relieved to be without her. And she *had* felt relief. After all of the holding and calming and whispering and shushing. It had been such a strain, a constant strain due to Shira's every creak and sneeze, her every swallow. Her chirp.

To be alone, even on the run, even in grave danger—yet without that extra needy weight, that other body on hers—was liberating. And oh. To eat. To eat anything and everything that she could find, without sparing, denying, saving, giving over.

The day she, Miri, and Chana stole meat from a villager's

smoker perched at the edge of the woods, she ate until her belly was full to bursting without regard for anything—not the villager's family, not the laws of kashruth—she's sure it was pig that she ate. It was only afterward that she considered how severely reduced the convent rations might have become. How her child could be near to starving and she hadn't thought to cache even a scrap of the preserved meat.

Róża paces the squat, unsettled, music pulsing in her head. She reaches for the found pen and paper. Turning the paper sideways, she lines it with staffs, adds in treble clefs and bass clefs. She scratches out notes—wholes, halves, quarters, eighths. Like everything else in this life, infinitely divisible.

She writes lines for cello and violin, interwoven like two fluid bodies that form a single, silent tangle in the hay, each note a star in the constellation of her life's anguish. She searches for Shira's face in the array.

Clouds plunge the room into semidarkness, all colors an octave lower. Róża stands up. As she does, she knocks over her tin cup of water, and the droplets set the ink to running: black notes drip down her legs, streak her shins, spot her toes. More agitated than ever, she heads once again for the streets.

Since the Russian soldiers came and left two days ago, the nuns hide, or they cluster together whispering, barely aware of the children.

Mother Agnieszka quakes terribly. Sister Alicja spends most of her time in her chamber. Sister Nadzieja huddles with the other nuns and forgets to come to Zosia's practice sessions. Not even Sister Olga checks to see that the girls are completing their chores.

When the sisters fail to prepare the day's lunch as they customarily do, Ula takes the lead and all the girls work together to make a platter of simple sandwiches. Adela plucks one off the top and eats it. Zosia carries a sandwich to Sister Alicja and feels pleased when she takes a bite. Watching her chew, slow and glassy-eyed, Zosia thinks how, in the barn, when Henryk brought her mother potatoes, she set most of them aside, sucking on hay despite the growling of her stomach, the jutting of her bones.

Zosia leaves Sister Alicja's chamber to help the girls with the laundry. She finds that a novitiate, Sister Irena, has emerged, ready to lead the chore. Together they work with quiet diligence, scrubbing red spots from the nuns' stiff underclothing.

This is not what she thought the end of the war would mean.

Through the fog of an early morning, Róża thinks she sees Aron standing at the convent site. Even if he is a phantom, she can't help herself from rushing toward him.

"Aron?"

"Różyczka!" His very real arms encircle her.

"How did you find me here?"

"Chana remembered the story you told about the convent address."

Róża buries her face in Aron's chest, inhaling him, hiding from him. What must he think of her, never uttering a word about Shira, then leaving to search for her without as much as a goodbye? She floods with guilty feelings. "Where is Chana?"

"She is with Hershel and some of the others, in Białystok. They planned to stay in Sonia's childhood home, but they are sleeping on the lawn because the inhabitants refuse to leave. It's all right—they're safe. And now I've found *you*." He takes her face in his hands. "Róża—"

Róża sees Aron surveying the rubble, but she clings to other visions: someone saw carriages by the convent, a line of girls along the cobbles.

"I have to keep looking."

Chapter 43

Autumn 1945

Zosia stares through the convent gates at the women walking past. One figure has her mother's narrow frame and dark hair, even her familiar gait. And one farther down the street looks to be wearing a dress like those her mother used to wear. Zosia detects a smile—could it be recognition?—on yet another's face. Until each comes closer and Zosia sees: they are strangers, merely.

In her disappointment, Zosia runs the back of her hand against the wrought-iron pickets. She traverses the length of the yard, clanging, until she is bruised and aching with a pain she'll feel most acutely later, when she raises up her violin and sends notes filled with melancholy into the reverberant air.

Zosia still plays every day—lately, both parts of "Rutén Kolomejka" from Bartók's 44 Duos, hers *and* Pan Skrzypczak's, wishing for him to come, to still be her teacher.

Sister Nadzieja explained, over and over, that he wasn't able to travel the distance to the new convent. Instead, after receiving Sister Nadzieja's letter about a donated gramophone, he sent several precious recordings with a note: *My dear Zosia: Listen to these well and they will teach you what you need to know.*

After practicing, Zosia puts on the recordings and listens—to Bach's Sonatas and Partitas or the Paganini 24 Caprices—while leafing through her workbooks and sheet music. Nearly every page has Pan Skrzypczak's neat pencil marks, notating changes in tempo or dynamics, emphasizing the rests. One particularly cherished page has a tiny smear of jam from the day he brought her a special cookie at Christmastime. Another looks to have tiny nibble marks at the edge, as if a mouse holed into her cabinet. The pages that still carry the piney, leather smells of Pan Skrzypczak's briefcase, the ones he brought her just prior to the move, she holds close to her nose and she floods with his presence.

In the careful, looping script the nuns taught her, Zosia writes a letter for Sister Nadzieja to post:

> *Dear Pan Skrzypczak,*
> *I don't think the motto Free but lonesome is any good.*
> *I listen to your recordings every day and I play best as I can but I don't improve without you. I miss our lessons terribly. Please, won't you come teach me?*
> *Your loving student,*
> *Zosia*

She waits anxiously for a letter in return.

One afternoon while Zosia cross-stitches pillow coverings with the other girls, a couple arrives and inquires after Mother Superior. The man wears a black coat and black hat; white fringes stick out beneath his shirt. Zosia recognizes the hunted look in his gray eyes.

"Are there any Jewish children here?"

"No, Rabbi." Mother Agnieszka's quick reply has gravel in it.

"Might I nevertheless be permitted to see the children of the orphanage?"

Mother Agnieszka hesitates, but the man strides over to where the girls are gathered. He stands before them and, as they go quiet, he sings.

> *Oyfn veg shteyt a boym,*
> *Ale feygl funem boym,*
> *Zaynen zikh tsefloygn.*

In his voice, Zosia hears the very sound of her mother, a melody that penetrates to her bones.

Perhaps she cries out, for as soon as it is over, the rabbi is deep in conversation with Mother Agnieszka, all the while gesturing toward Zosia.

Zosia scrambles to her feet. "Do you know my mother?" she asks him. Before he can answer, she turns to Mother Agnieszka. "*Does* he?"

Mother Agnieszka's face furrows. She wraps Zosia in an embrace, then lets her go and turns briskly away. The rabbi takes Zosia's hand in his. She keeps hold of it, dry but soft, and inhales the stale wool smell of his coat.

That afternoon, Zosia is packed up to go. She is told that she will finally be with her own people.

"My mother? Do you mean I will be with my mother?"

In every dream in which she leaves the convent, Zosia is nestled in her mother's arms. What if she is supposed to wait here for her? Uncertain, she goes to stand before the stone statue of Mary and, for several minutes, presses her fingers to the carved folds of Mary's robes. Kasia finds Zosia there and clings to her. Zosia clings back.

When Sister Alicja comes for her, Zosia breaks into sobs. She doesn't understand where she is going. Can't they bring her mother here? Why must she leave the people who care for her? Why must she let go of her truest friend?

As Sister Alicja ushers Zosia through the front hall, several sisters are gathered in the corridor, talking.

"How can it be better for her to be taken away from here, to be placed among strangers?"

"All I know is they have been annihilated. They must reclaim whoever is left."

"But why *her*? She's just one child! They speak of sending her to Palestine!"

There is a shuffle on the stair.

"Sister Olga, are you crying? For *Zosia*?"

"I was frightened. God forgive me, I know there was no excuse for my nosing around. Poor girl, where are they taking her?"

"We don't know. We must trust in God's will."

Sisters Alicja and Nadzieja huddle around the carriage and take turns squeezing Zosia tight. Choking back tears, Sister Alicja loops the toggle buttons at the collar of Zosia's coat. Sister Nadzieja hands Zosia a large duffel, the little violin concealed inside, to take with her.

It is only dusk, but already the moon is out. Zosia's heart clamors. She reaches for her braid.

"Am I going to be with my mother?" Zosia asks.

Again the two nuns hug her, burying their faces in their sleeves. *They* have been like mothers, caring for her, giving her what she needs.

Again, Zosia bursts into tears.

In the coach, Zosia sits sniffling and puffy eyed beside the rabbi's wife. Head scarf drawn tight, she seeks to soothe Zosia with a hand on her arm, her eyes soft. But with Sisters Alicja and Nadzieja turning back at the convent gate, Zosia feels a rising panic. *Am I being taken to my mother or to strangers, like Sister Irena said?*

With a jerky start, the carriage begins its ramble over the uneven cobblestones, away from the convent building. The rabbi's wife hums another melody that is familiar. Zosia cups her hands in her lap, wishing for the comfort of her bird amid all the confusion. But in her mind, her bird has grown larger, fiercer. His bright yellow feathers appear coarse and gray, and his feet boast sharp talons. His call is neither a melodious eighteen-note wonder nor a tremulous wavering between two notes. It is a strident warning shriek.

Zosia wakes, shivering, with the rabbi's wife still beside her in the carriage. It is entirely dark except for a thin strip of light bleeding in at the curtain's edge. Zosia yanks the curtain aside and sees that they are stopped outside a large encampment with lanterns illuminating a path to a doorway.

"Where am I going?"

"Don't worry, dear. You'll stay here just until we can secure safe passage to your homeland."

Does this mean I am going home? Am I here first, to find my mother?

The rabbi's wife leads Zosia, clasping tight to her duffel,

up the path. Inside, a large room is subdivided by blankets hanging from the ceiling. Along the corridor, the air reeks of sweat and soured milk. A baby yowls from within. Lifting the sides of blankets and peering in, the rabbi's wife disturbs several families getting settled for the night before she locates the orphan unit and, within it, an empty bed. She pats the covers, indicating for Zosia to get in.

"You're to be called Tzofia from now on. Don't worry, you can be yourself here—everyone is just like you."

She feels even lonelier than when she looked down the row of convent beds to see Adela and Ula and the other girls. For the first time she considers *their* loneliness—Ula, orphaned at age three; Adela, left at the convent door despite rumors that her parents still lived in the outskirts of Celestyn. Above all she misses Kasia, who showed her whipped cream in the clouds, skating floors in newly polished wood, and holy expressions in the faces of cats; who from her first "hallo" treated her, always, as her friend.

She tosses in bed for hours. With another new name, she is a stranger to herself again. She suddenly, desperately longs for her blanket, with its bumpy stitched seam. *Why didn't I think to take it?*

She gets up and wanders through the corridor. Peering through a streaked window, she sees it is early morning. In a dirt area between low-slung barracks, children chase one another in packs, racing and climbing in the branches of a lone tree. The sky is overcast, gray. Tzofia puts her hands to the cold glass.

Farther down the corridor, a cluster of women circle a woodstove in a room cluttered with mismatched chairs, trunks, and stacks of books. From the doorway, Tzofia studies the lines on the women's faces, the expressions in their eyes. She watches for the tilt of their heads, listens for the lilt in their voices. She finds no trace of her mother.

At mealtime, Tzofia follows the children to a dining hall and watches as the adults gather to eat, hats and skullcaps and kerchiefs upon their heads. No signing of the cross but, instead, shawls around shoulders and heads bowed in prayer. She feels lost here, where children run loose and the day unspools without regimens or rules. She misses the confines of the convent wall; she misses the church songs and rituals, her days structured around morning and evening prayers. Under her breath, Tzofia says grace over her food and barely touches it.

As the eaters disperse, a bony, hollow woman grabs hold of Tzofia's shoulder and looks wildly into her eyes. She smells of salt and singed nuts; the flesh above her left cheek quivers. Tzofia can see that the woman is lost, too, drowning in her own hopes.

"Is it you, my daughter? Can it be?"

The woman's confusion matches Tzofia's. She stares into the woman's eyes. They are wrong: not the color of midnight. "No!" Tzofia shouts.

"My sweet Rachel?"

"Let me go!"

If Tzofia is certain of anything, it is that she is not this woman's daughter. She fights to break away from the woman's tight grasp and haunted gaze.

Tzofia runs across a muddy path and enters a building filled with classroom desks and chairs and more strangers. On the chalkboard, words in other languages: Hebrew and English. She wants to get out of this place! If she can't be with her mother, she wants to be with Sister Alicja and Sister

Nadzieja, who care for her. She peers through the doorway. A cloud of blackbirds darkens the sky.

The scary woman totters away.

Later in the evening, a crowd congregates around a bonfire and the singing starts. Tzofia once again hears the long-ago songs, songs her mother sang to her at bedtime in Gracja and whispered to her in the barn. She leans in, surveying the faces, old and young, around the circle. *Who are these people, and how do they know my mother's songs?*

The singing rattles her even as it pulses in her veins. She covers her ears and imagines the ringing Latin chants of the convent. She closes her eyes to see the chapel in its hushed glory, the sisters gathered in the sanctuary, kneeling, praying for their protection. She wonders about her communion service: Was it real, or was it just Mother Agnieszka's way to keep her safe?

In an effort to soothe herself, Tzofia retrieves her violin. She bends one finger and then another to the strings, her bow moving slowly as she locates the notes, just as she did in the convent classroom with Sister Nadzieja standing beside her, listening. She lets herself be guided by the swell of voices around her, and soon there are no individual notes, no separable lines of melody or harmony. Tzofia is tucked in the nest of her bed quilt, her parents kissing her cheeks with gentle mama bird and *tata* bird pecks. She is in the barn loft, her father already gone but her mother there, breath and sweat mingled with hay. She is in the doorway of the barn, her arms extended, reaching out for her mother's hands. One by one, the singers around the fire trail off as the haunted tones of Tzofia's violin articulate the displacement that, together, they share.

From that night on, Tzofia plays to see the chestnut hues in her mother's black hair, the lines around her father's eyes. Her memories more distinct, her thoughts grow less dissonant, as she continues to play. She remembers a dinner of chicken paprikash—the tips of her grandmother's fingers were tinged red for two days afterward—and staying up past midnight, her eyes transfixed on her mother's vibrating wrist as she pressed her fingers to the strings of her cello. No scared whispering that night, but she could feel the distress in her mother's playing and in the off-tempo bounce of her grandfather's knee. Her father didn't even take up his violin, he just paced the room, and her grandmother took to cleaning top to bottom, polishing the wooden sideboard with extra vigor. All of them acted as if they'd forgotten her bedtime, but she sensed that they preferred to be together, huddled in the tight space of the parlor.

In time, she becomes known not as the girl who plays the violin but as *the violinist*. An elderly man named Yizhai, hunched and graying and smelling faintly of cabbage, claims her for his own.

"How is my little violinist?" he asks her whenever they pass, giving a slight bow of his head. Tzofia smiles a wordless reply.

Maybe Tzofia would never be one for words. But horsehair on string, bow-arm at just the right angle, with her violin, all that Tzofia holds inside floats out of her in long, even strokes. Rather than the mass of her own body, rather than words, choked and dry, it is the heft of the violin upon her shoulder, the smooth rest for her chin, the steady pressure demanded of her hand on the bow, that roots Tzofia in the world.

Chapter 44

Aron and Róża stand outside Celestyn's Carmelite church at noon. It is Aron's idea, since the central committee has no records on Shira and the town officials seem not to know anything. As churchgoers leave mass, Aron approaches and asks what they know about the bombed convent. Some walk past without answering. But a nun brightens at the mention of the Felicjanki.

"I believe they are staying with the Siostry Nazaretanki," she says.

Róża's *"Really?"* comes out at the same time as Aron's *"Where?"*

"Last I heard, they'll be hosted there until their convent can be rebuilt, or—"

"Do you know if any children moved with them?" Róża asks.

"I imagine so; there was a recent communion."

"Communion?"

"Can you tell us where?"

"The Nazareth's nunnery is on ul. Swiętokrzyska at the far limit of Celestyn."

* * *

They begin walking right away. Curled leaves rustle about
their feet, blanketing the char and rubble. It is dusk by the
time they reach the gate. Róża clasps the iron bars, cold
on her fingers. Aron rings the bell. After a few minutes,
a young nun habited with an all-white headdress and high
boots comes over.

"May I help you?"

"We are searching for my daughter, Shira Chodorów,"
Róża blurts.

"Who?"

Róża's shame catches in her throat. "She . . . had a different name, I don't—"

"I think I'd better get Mother Agnieszka."

While they wait, Róża stares at a garden patch, tightly
pruned and browning. When an older nun shuffles toward
them, her heavy robes rustling, it distresses Róża to see a
tremor in her face. As if, already, she is saying *No*.

"I'm Mother Agnieszka."

"My daughter . . ." Róża swallows. "I didn't realize she
could have survived in the woods. . . ." She begins again. "In
the barn, she was always humming and tapping. And when
we were made to leave . . . I was given this card. I've come
now . . ."

Róża stops. She sees a flicker of understanding, perhaps
the recognition of their resemblance; then a downcast look
in Mother Agnieszka's eyes.

"I am terribly sorry. A rabbi and his wife offered to secure
her a more appropriate placement. They were leaving, too. I
thought it was best for Zosia to be among her people."

Róża utters the name: "*Zosia*." Aron is silent.

A different nun, who had drawn near, then rushed away,

comes to them now with a garden spade in one hand, something disinterred in the other. "There was a particular spot near the hedges she visited often—when I saw the rock, I had a hunch she buried this there. I regret that I didn't dig it up for *her.*"

Róża recognizes Shira's shred of blanket, limp and soil covered. With tears streaming from her eyes, she takes it and holds it close, sniffing in vain for the faded scent of her child. She smells the rooted earth.

"We pray for her every day. We pray that she is safe," the sister says.

Mother Agnieszka does not stop shaking.

Tzofia is absorbed in her practice session—her legs driven firmly into the ground, rooted, her whole self thickening—when Rifka interrupts her. Rifka is Tzofia's same age, here with her parents and their goose in tow, after escaping the Lublin ghetto and waiting out the war on a farm that the Germans overlooked. Rifka knows the camp's routines inside and out: each afternoon at two P.M., Marian brings cookies to the children's room; Aniela teaches her special art class on Tuesdays; and the fresh milk delivery happens now! She begs Tzofia to come. They can slip in through the kitchen's back entry and each have a glass.

Tzofia lets herself be led there. Rifka presses open the swing door and they slip into the space, much larger than the convent kitchens, humid but clean, lined with metal racks of dry dishes. While Tzofia watches, Rifka carefully pours two glasses of milk and hands one to Tzofia.

"My parents say that we will soon travel by boat to a better land. You'll come too, won't you?"

Tzofia shrugs. With the glass at her lips, she inhales the

milk's rangy smell, tastes the cool froth. It reminds her of
the cups of honeyed milk her grandmother gave her before
bed; the clink of glasses when she and her mother "toasted"
their shared birthdays before devouring large triangular
slices of cake; the feel of Krystyna's arm on her shoulder,
patiently showing her how to pat the cows on their long sides.
She slurped up the cows' sweet milk, still warm despite the
chilled tin cup, as many times as Krystyna would refill it,
marveling all the while at the animals' freedom to make
whatever noise they liked. Then, returning to the loft, she
hesitated, her eyes reluctant to adjust to the dimness and
dusk, her body resistant to being stifled and stilled. She
wanted to be back with her mother—she did—but she did
not want to be swallowed up by the barn's silence.

As she thinks of it, Tzofia's chest goes tight and she gulps
for air. She leaves Rifka and walks back to the practice room,
its window still open a crack. She reaches for her violin.

Bow to string. It is the only way Tzofia knows to converse
with the silences life has made her companions. Always, she
begins her practice with the lullaby her mother sang to her
in the barn: *Cucuricoo! Di mom iz nisht do . . .* She moves
on to Brahms's Scherzo, then assorted pieces she learned
with Pan Skrzypczak. Bartók's Rhapsodies no. 1 and no. 2;
Rimsky-Korsakov's "Flight of the Bumblebee." The jumpy
bow strokes remind her acutely of her bird, his tremulous
two-note call. She looks around for something new.

Tzofia sorts through the box of music that someone journeyed with here, prized above other worldly possessions. She
finds a piece by Ravel, *Kaddish*, for violin and piano. She
scans the score, then starts to play through the melody, stopping many times to get each tone, each articulation, exactly

right. When she feels she has it, she plays from the beginning, filling in the piano in her head as she goes.

The melody—its slowness, its tender sadness, the way each note seems both tense and peaceful at the same time—reminds Tzofia of music her father played. At first, the piano gives only the sparest accompaniment, its high notes ringing out distantly, shimmering crystal-like alongside Tzofia's melody. But the piano's part soon grows richer, circling Tzofia's music with arpeggiations, embracing it like two bodies entwined. Tzofia remembers herself in the barn with her mother, lying in the hay, silent, music in her head. Only now she's singing her melody out loud, and her mother's dark eyes shine encouragingly. She quickens her tempo a bit, letting each note lean forward expectantly, and she sways with the ebb and flow of her music. Her tone grows warmer, more joyful. In the piano's chords she hears consolation, like a hand extended. Tzofia and her mother walk together, out of the barn, through the garden and the field . . .

A single chord lands uncertain, as if hesitant, stopping to make up its mind. It comes so unexpectedly that Tzofia wonders if it's a mistake, but the next chord in the piano clarifies: it is determined, turning away, going back. *Where?*

Tzofia's melody rises, as if in protest, as the piano's music becomes darker, deeper. Tzofia unfolds her melody in long waves that swell and crest with yearning, while the piano sinks further, further into its depths, until it's just a quiet rumble, the echo of a distant cry. With the piano far away, Tzofia's delicate melody plays its own sad arpeggiations, each reaching higher than the last. She tilts her body out again, she brings her violin into the air, her music becomes bolder. As if in response, the piano strains across its keys to reach chords, quiet but ecstatic, that bridge the distance between the instruments, touching the melody one last time. Tzofia holds on to her final note as long as she can, until her bow slides imperceptibly from motion to stillness, from sound to silence.

In the score sitting before her, the piano ends where it began, the same invocatory note ringing like a bell, as if in an endless cycle. But Tzofia plays the piece through only once, holding her bow on her string long after she has stopped playing, her eyes closed.

Outside, the call of birds.

The nuns pray for Zosia every day because, as rumor has it, Jews from across Europe crowd illegally into cargo ships bound for Palestine and meet with detentions, diversions to other ports, even bombs buried within.

Róża grows shaky to think of it. Shira survived the bombings; she was here, safe and sound. Yet the only remaining trace is her blanket, dug up from beneath the privet by a sister who kept closest watch. Róża grips it tight.

She continues searching. At a refugee center, she is given the address of the nearest displaced persons camps. One in particular seems to be the favorite of Bricha workers who "rescue" surviving Jewish children from Christian homes. Maybe this is where the rabbi and his wife have taken Shira?

Upon arriving there, Róża searches the faces of the children huddled around picnic tables. She walks through a yard where other children play tag. She inquires at the office.

"No records with the name Chodorów. No Shiras or Zosias, either. Could it have been changed?"

"It was Zosia when she was in the orphanage."

"Maybe she's taken on a different name."

"Can I please look at all the names you have on your list?"

"You can, but between you and me, our records aren't great. We do our best, but with all the comings and goings— people arrive here in the middle of the night, and if there's word of a possible transport from Hamburg, they depart suddenly and without notice. In just the past weeks, I've heard of boats heading to Palestine, New York, and Morocco. Waves have come and gone. It's hard to keep up."

"Is there a child here who is especially musical?"

"Excuse me?"

"Musical. Always humming and tapping."

"There was a girl who played violin at the campfire. A real talent. But she left last week, to where, I don't know. Never talked much, but she sure could play."

Róża asks around about the campfire violinist. Everyone speaks of a quiet child around the age of eight or nine, who played like a virtuoso.

"I never heard anyone like her, and so young!" one older man tells Róża.

"There was a family with a child her age she hung around; maybe they took her with them?" the man's wife chimes in.

"Do you know the name of that family?"

"No."

"Or where they may have gone?"

"I'm sorry."

Róża and Aron travel to Hamburg Port. Róża searches the boat records; she stands on the docks and stares out at the heaving sea. They may have passed within ten kilometers of each other as Róża traveled west from Celestyn and

Shira traveled north from the camp to the port. They may have missed each other by a matter of *days*. Now there is no knowing where Shira has gone to.

Aron's face registers Róża's despondency. "Oh, Różyczka."

Wherever Shira is, she won't be traceable now. He doesn't say it, but they both know: Shira is lost to the universe.

They circle the city on foot, directionless. The air from Róża's lungs gets stoppered in her throat. If she could hold out hope that Shira would search for *her*—but would Shira even know her name?

Aron wipes tears from her eyes and brings water for her to drink. He sits beside her on a bench. A solitary goldfinch whirls overhead.

"Róża, *please*. Honor Shira by living a beautiful life."

Róża blinks up at the sky as Aron takes hold of her hands.

Part 4

The girl does not need to be silent any longer, so she plays her music out loud. She plays, not for the flowers that grow in colorful clay pots on her terrace or for a distant, long-ago garden. She plays for the airwaves. Her notes travel at the speed of three hundred and thirty-two meters per second, faster even than a yellow bird.

After longest silence, she wishes for her music to reach as high as the heavens, as far as the sea.

Chapter 45

New York
Autumn 1965

Róża pulls two knit blankets from a high shelf, spreading one across the bed, the other on the couch; then she transfers her thick sweaters, individually wrapped in plastic bags, to the middle drawers of her dressing closet. Autumn's chill has come early to Brooklyn this year, but it's all right. Their apartment is cozy, and in the evenings, when she and Aron stroll the neighborhood and talk, vendors stand ready on street corners with her favorite roasted chestnuts nestled in paper cones.

She climbs a step stool to retrieve the woolen coats and hats to be traded out with the lighter things in the front closet. Then she tidies up the music room, what might have been a child's room, though she and Aron don't talk about *that*. The one time she got pregnant here—not far along; she didn't even suspect until the spotting began—her body just couldn't hold on to it. She let herself bleed out, crouched over the toilet, her head pressed against the cool metal of the towel rack, silent and still as if she were yet in hiding, overcome once again by the scent of rust and rot.

She knew then that she couldn't bear another child—where

would the necessary light come from, after the burials beneath hay, snow, rabbit, rubble?—and so with discretion she avoided Aron on her most fertile days, and they played aunt and uncle to Chana and Hershel's four children. The curve of the children's cheeks, the pudge of their arms, the translucence of their fingers, it all stung, and it was only after the youngest surpassed five—Shira's age in the barn—that Róża could wholly embrace them, despite the regular Friday night dinners and birthday celebrations. With her own birthday just two days apart from Shira's, family picnics on the Narew River stirred within her: how Shira covered her eyes and fidgeted with anticipation, waiting for the cello song to start, then exclaiming over her grandmother's cakes, frosted like jeweled castles, each year more beautiful than the last.

Sometimes, visualizing her girl's luminous face, or poring over her old photograph, now framed atop her bureau, Róża thinks maybe beauty *can* save the world. But then something cuts in. The liquid brown of a girl's eyes at the grocery counter, or a snippet of music—a violin solo on the radio—shakes her to her fault lines. A long-buried memory ambushes her. She'd turned crazy with anguish immediately after Shira was taken from the barn. When Henryk and Krystyna stepped inside, she fell into Krystyna's arms, crying. Her girl was gone from her. Gone from all of them—

For dinner, she makes meat loaf and wedge salad. That's what's featured in the magazines here. Later, she'll walk with Aron to the nearest Italian bakery, where they'll share a cannoli, taking smaller and smaller bites, in turn, until it's gone.

Emerging from a past life means embracing new things,

steering away from reminders. Not scanning the faces of passersby on walks; not returning to the library, again, to search the records; not rummaging through the bottom of a trunk to feel for a tattered shred of blanket, an old watch and compass, a small card with an address printed on it.

Of the reminders Róża skirts here in Greenpoint—the Jewish bakery cases packed with babka and rugelach; certain dress shop windows; any recipe containing mushrooms—one exception is the cello. First rented, now owned, Róża plays and teaches. She accepts students at least ten years or older, a steadfast rule. Not the young ones; never the kindergarten prodigies. The teenagers, lanky and impressionable, she finds most endearing: how they dress in their sturdy jeans and speak in their perfect English, raving about their favorite American rock idols even as they rehearse their measures by Haydn and Beethoven and Bach. After trudging up the tight stairs to the apartment, they settle into a chair in the music room, shifting into a sun puddle by the bay window, wrangling their cellos between their legs. Róża encourages them through their warm-ups and exercises: open string bowing, left hand pizzicati, double stops for the advanced students.

She listens to music—broadcasts on WQXR—whenever she has the chance. She knits as she listens, often thinking of the way her father hummed along to recordings as he meticulously crafted his violins.

Today, she tunes in late to a solo violinist playing Szymanowski's *Mythes*. She settles with her needles and yarn—her newest project: a winter scarf in blue bouclé—and her Lipton tea.

Delicate and shimmering, the violinist's notes displace her from the start. The music unfolds in lines of tension and calm, water flowing, then still, a wooded night turning to dawn. Past memories surface like rising water. Róża might be back in Gracja, by the riverbank, Natan beside her, Shira's tiny fingers tapping upon her *bobe*'s leg. But soon the sound grows haunted, and she and Shira are running from all they know and love, huddling together, holding tight. In the music's dusky timbres she hears the song of the barn rafters, the moistening hay, the night sky. Memories that save as they destroy.

Late in the afternoon, her students arrive. First Stanley, then Muriel.

The last of the day is Julie, her star student. Julie troops in, her cello pressed against her hip, her school bag dangling behind her, the sugary scent of a powdered doughnut still on her lips. Before tuning up, she presses back the fringe of her hair with a thick white headband. Her bright expression turns concerted and serious as she bends toward her strings, sounding notes and listening, subtly adjusting the pegs. Next year, she will attend the Juilliard program for high schoolers.

For an hour straight, they work on the Glazunov *Concerto Ballata*. When Julie packs up to leave, she says, "I have a ticket for next Sunday's violin concert at Carnegie Hall, but because of the Bach chamber audition, I can't go! The seat's up front, though off to the side. Would you like it?"

"Yes, I'd love it. Thank you."

Later, Róża calls the box office to buy a second ticket for Aron, but the concert is sold out.

Chapter 46

Tzofia spends long days in a practice room at Heichal HaTarbut. She doesn't break for a snack or even a brief walk outside; she works concertedly on her recital pieces, measure by measure, her eyes fixed on the wall, streaked by the tines of metal music stands and the backs of folding chairs. To this day she marks the progress of her practice sessions with coins—five shekels crossing the length of a side shelf or else slid back and starting all over again—to master her playing free of mistakes.

Her talents were discovered here when a violoncellist from the Palestine Orchestra heard her playing at a campfire at the kibbutz Neve Ora. He urged the musical director, still looking to fill spots, to come hear her, and it was he who arranged for her advanced training. Now, so many years later and a first violinist with the Israel Philharmonic Orchestra, she practices "Dryades et Pan," part of the program she recently recorded and will perform, along with the Brahms Scherzo, live next Tuesday in London and the following Sunday in New York.

She goes by Tzofia Levy now. Journeying here with Rivka's family, she adopted their surname. Her given name, lost with her blanket, no longer rattles inside her; and the urge to search for her mother, each time it arises, is quashed by the fact that she does not know her mother's name either. Years earlier, just before her own daughter, Shoshana, was born, she tried to discover it. At Yad Vashem, she stared at the inscription: *To them I will give within my temple and its walls a memorial and a name better than sons and daughters.* . . . Despite searching through survivor records and Żegota transport lists, she couldn't unearth it.

She did locate an address for Pan Skrzypczak and wrote, thanking him for all he taught her. He replied, a long letter—the marks on the page transporting her to Mother Agnieszka's chamber, his figure bent over music pages, etching notes in dark pencil. In the letter he expressed his great relief for her survival and safety, his delight in the successes he knew she was capable of. All his dearness flooded back to her with his insistence that *she* had taught *him* the more. He wished to see her perform, and she was preparing to mail him a ticket to an upcoming concert in Vienna when she got word of his death. In unguarded moments it still makes her ache and stirs thoughts of reconnecting with Kasia, and Sisters Alicja and Nadzieja, who cared for her— but she has no wish to return to Poland. She stays pointed forward, focusing on her family, her music.

Looking at her watch, she startles to see that it's nearly five o'clock. She packs her violin into its case, slings it over her back, and steps outside.

Rothschild Boulevard is crowded, the air sticky and hot. She stops at a market, buys almond paste, butter, and lemons, then continues walking. She wants to get a cake in the oven before dinnertime. Not lavish or ornate, but her daughter's favorite: almond cake topped with cream and fresh raspberries. Tomorrow they'll go to Meir Garden for a small party. Tzofia will feel a jab in the low of her stomach as she plays "HaYom Yom Huledet" on her violin and tells the story of a little girl and her bird who gather daisies for a fancy birthday garland, marking the day her daughter turns five years old.

In the subway, no Sunday crowds, Róża stands, one arm looped around a metal pole. Across the aisle, a little girl with long braids sits gripping the bunched fabric of her brother's pant leg. Róża peers at her reflection in the window glass. When the train pulls into the Fifty-seventh Street station, she hustles out toward the concert hall.

Inside, Róża hands her ticket to a thin-lipped lady in a high-collared blouse and weaves down the carpeted aisle. She's been to Carnegie Hall only a handful of times, once to hear Janos Starker. She turns circles in the auditorium, marveling at the gilded columns, the high-arched ceilings. She drops into her velvet-covered seat, clutching the concert program.

Couples in black-tie dress, row upon row of them, tip toward each other and talk. They smell of cologne and pomade and clothes starch. Róża feels shabby in her simple dress. She sits upright, solitary, her coat tight around her, and stares ahead at the stage, set with metal chairs and music stands.

Róża remembers a long-ago night in her parents' parlor, she and Natan tuning up their strings. They'd planned to practice Ravel's Sonata for Violin and Cello together, but then Natan winked—a change in plan—and went off on a Gypsy riff, a fiddling frenzy. Shira, who was nestled between her grandparents, blanket in hand, wriggled from her perch and began running in circles, sheet music fluttering from the stands as she whooshed by. Róża set aside her cello and ran after Shira, catching her, curling her to her chest. Her parents rose also, and they all began dancing, twirling in the tight space of the room, the Gypsy music pulsing through them. Hot and happy. Panting.

Chapter 47

When she steps onto the stage, Tzofia looks out over the tight rows of seats, extending upward in lit balcony circles. She joins her pianist for a bow, puts her ear to her violin to tune. Then she closes her eyes, taking in the hushed silence of the hall, and imagines her first notes in her head: the rapping opening, sounds connected with her earliest memories—silence and confusion, but also warmth and touch—which she aims to infuse into every note.

As always when she performs, no matter where around the world, she angles face out beneath the glare. Just before bringing her bow-arm down upon string, she scans the visible rows and allows herself to imagine.

Off to the side, a woman with midnight eyes.

On the woman's shoulder, a tiny yellow bird.

The music rises as if from the ground beneath Róża's feet, pulsing through hay and feathers and white rubble. The violin's rapping, a pounding in her chest; the piano's rising chords, a restless cry. Notes that Róża once scrawled on hand-drawn staffs, once whispered in the silence of the barn's high loft, now rush back to her across the hall, across the years: Brahms's Scherzo reverberating in her every cell like the longing that precedes all memory.

The violin pours out the melody of soulful exultation. Grounded by the piano's chords, its song swoops from high, generously, tenderly, like the folding of a hand. When the violin and piano switch parts, the violinist plays the accompaniment in soft, rising phrases, each ending higher than the last and trailing off like a searching, unfinished thought. Róża feels herself straightening up in her seat as if to catch the music in the air, lifted by each ascent, wishing to cry out yet staying silent.

The romping start returns, a wild gallop as the piano accelerates, its pitch higher and higher, then stops suddenly as if it has finally reached its destination; and now the violin sings the joyous middle theme. Róża can't see for her tears as the music tells her all she needs to know: they were as one, from seed within womb to bodies entangled beneath hay to beings apart yet with melodies—*this* melody—shared between them, always.

The ending comes as a gift, a surprise placed into cupped hands, expressing affection so powerful as to banish all loneliness. Note by note it thickens like glass beads on a strand.

Róża stands up.

With the final chord, Tzofia lets her bow-arm drop and brings her violin to her side. Amid the audience's applause, she smiles at her pianist and bows.

Patrons rustle, about to start rising from their seats. One, off to the side, is already standing. Tzofia blinks against the stagelights and looks in her direction, faint hope fluttering inside her, like a yellow bird flying its way home.

Note About Polish Surnames

In the Polish language, surnames sometimes take different gender forms and so have different endings. Thus the surname of a married woman can have a different ending than the surname of her husband. I have abided by this convention here. Titles, such as "Mr." (*Pan*) and "Mrs." (*Pani*), and surnames can vary in form depending on sentence case. To avoid confusion for English-language readers, I have written all such titles and surnames in nominative form.

Translations

Nightly lullaby (from Yiddish):
Cucuricoo!
Mama isn't here.
Where has she gone?
To get a glass of tea,
Who is going to drink it?
You and me. (switched to rhyme)

Mourner's prayer that Róża recites for Miri (from Hebrew):
May His great name grow exalted and sanctified
in the world that He created as He willed.
May He give reign to His Kingship
in your lifetime and in your days,
and in the lifetimes of the entire Family of
Israel . . .

Folk song that the rabbi sings in the convent (from Yiddish):
On the path there stands a tree,
it stands there bowed,
all birds from that tree
have flown away.

Acknowledgments

Amy Einhorn, editor extraordinaire, saw into the heart of this project and, with great insight and trust, helped me to develop it. Conor Mintzer provided brilliant comments about plot and language, perfectly attuned to the work's emotional pulse. Francesca Main at Picador and the wonderful Flatiron team, especially Bob Miller, Caroline Bleeke, Amelia Possanza, Nancy Trypuc, Cristina Gilbert, Katherine Turro, and Keith Hayes, gave this book wings into the larger world. Gail Hochman championed my writing—and even offered a bat mitzvah! Jennifer Einhorn always believed in this story and I am beyond grateful to her.

It was my privilege and honor to interview Stan Berger, Myra Genn, Roald Hoffmann, Millie Selinger, Ruth Salton, and the late George Salton. Your life stories, filled with bravery, perseverance, ingenuity, and love, inspire my awe. While the characters and events in this book are fictional, our conversations enriched me and every page I've written.

My Poland guide, Paweł Szczerkowski, along with Rafał Brenner and Tomasz Ciemiorek, took me to the settings of my imagination and brought historical depth, cultural richness, and fun to our journey. In Israel, Amnon Weinstein welcomed me into his workshop, where he painstakingly restores violins once played by Jews in ghettos and camps for concerts of commemoration and hope.

If the relationship between Shira and her teacher is dear, it is perhaps because the relationships I've had with my teachers and mentors have been all the dearer: Marilyn Abildskov, you have understood me as a writer from the start, and I am so grateful for your perceptiveness, generosity, and intelligence about life's ordinary moments; thank you, Lan Samantha Chang, for your keen sense of a story's pacing and its beating heart; Tony Doerr, for your limitless curiosity about the universe and the sheer beauty of your sentences; David Russell, for your unbounded enthusiasm for music, this project, and your treasure trove of anecdotes; Michelle Wildgen, for your deep understanding of narrative cause and effect; Steven Bauer, for your trustworthy narrative intuitions and your ongoing encouragement; Kevin McIlvoy, for your wisdom about books and life and for your constant faith in my creativity.

Linda Wentworth brought me all the right resources. Catherine Epstein helped me with the history and more. Demetrius Shahmehri taught me how to listen for the stories inside the music. Dusty Miller and Marc Fromm read for a child's mind, trauma, and dreams. Kent Hicks taught me about tracking—and also built the house where I wrote some of this! Pamela Erens showed me that important changes can be made even to a nearly baked cake. Susan O'Neill shed light on convent life. Martha Scherzer and Jonathan Vatner brainstormed with me at one of my lowest points and brought steady, insightful thinking. This manuscript is better because of Rebecca Gradinger's great story instincts.

Thank you to many dear, loving friends: for reading for me at the earliest, worst stages and still encouraging me to continue on: Julia Mintz, Brittany Shahmehri, Catherine Newman, Katryna Nields, Sara Just, Missy Wick, Jean Zimmer, Alisa Greenbacher, Tamar Naor, Tracy Camenisch, Gideon Yaffe, Chris Cander, Judith Frank, Naomi Shulman, Carol Edelstein, Robin Barber, Linda Moore, Amanda Roach, Cynthia Gensheimer, and Shelley Nolden. For fortifying visits, walks, meals, and endless tea drinking: Emily Neuburger, Lydia Peterson, Claudia Canale-Parola, Becky Michaels, Judith Inglese, Ariana Inglese, Kristin Rotas, Anne Hulley, Suzanne Forman, Caryn Brause, Steve Breslow, Drew and Cathy Starkweather, Lauren Weinsier, Jennifer Addas, and Nancy Garlock. And further afield but no less dear: Cathy Bendor, Matthew Tarran, Jennine Kirby, Keith and Lisa Lucas, Manuel and Stephanie Vargas, Susan Verducci, Jenny Walter, Lisa McLeod, Vance Ricks, Susan Leeds, Sarah Buss, and Mar Corning.

I am thankful for the Tin House Summer Workshop, the Bread Loaf Writers' Conference, and the Iowa Summer Writing Festival, and for uninterrupted writing time at Wellspring House, Patchwork Farm, and Hillside House.

Thank you to my family, the Rosners, Corwins, and Malinas: there is a string connecting us always, and I love you. (Nancy: You helped to keep me healthy. Elisa: You helped to keep me sane!)

Goldie and Rosebud: Our river walks were, perhaps, the key here.

Bill, Sophia, and Juliet: You lived through the writing and rewriting of every word in this book, and you never wavered in your encouragement. My love for you surpasses infinity, and I am thankful every day that you are my home.

Author's Note

Several years ago, I was at a book event for *If a Tree Falls*, my memoir about raising our deaf daughters in a hearing, speaking world. A woman in the audience relayed her childhood experience during World War II: She was hidden with her mother in an attic, where she needed to stay silent nearly all of the time. I imagined the mother's experience of trying to keep her young child hushed, an effort exactly *opposite* mine, which focused on encouraging my children to vocalize as much as possible.

Afterward I arranged to meet with the woman, a "hidden child," as she called herself, and through her connections, I met several more. Soon I found myself immersed in a new project involving silence, separation, loss, and, above all, love.

Some of the hidden children I met were placed in hiding apart from their families. I was overwhelmed by their persisting hurt at this separation—despite knowing that it was for the sake of their survival. Some were given new names and placed in Christian settings; many had difficulty, after the war, recovering a sense of community and identity.

At the U.S. Holocaust Memorial Museum there are pamphlets with a child's photo and the caption *Remember me?*

The question is meant to be literal: If you remember me, if there is anyone out there who recognizes me and can tell me about my family, my name, then I might discover my history, my roots: my self. For refugees of current wars and violence, children displaced and torn from their families, this question echoes on.

My own childhood was marked, daily, by the sound of my father practicing the violin. During the writing of this book, I had the opportunity to meet an Israeli luthier who was asked to rebuild a violin recovered from a Nazi death camp, ashes still inside it. I listened to the sounds of other war-salvaged violins, and felt as if I were hearing the distinct voices of their lost players. I knew, then, that the girl in my story would be musical, that music would be something she shared with her family, together and apart.

The Yellow Bird Sings is a story about longing: the longing of a child and her mother to be connected, to be heard, to find their way home. I dedicate it to my parents.

Praise for *The Yellow Bird Sings*

National Jewish Book Award Finalist

"Rosner's exquisite, heart-rending debut novel is proof that there's always going to be room for another story about World War II . . . This is an absolutely beautiful and necessary novel, full of heartbreak but also hope, about the bond between mother and daughter, and the sacrifices made for love."
—*The New York Times*

"Jennifer Rosner hooks readers from the onset . . . Readers will have empathy for Róża and Shira, and admire Róża's courage and persistence as she faces life without her daughter, releasing her to save her, like a bird freed from a cage."
—*The Missourian*

"Prepare to have your heart broken."
—*Good Housekeeping*

"The Yellow Bird Sings is at the top of my reading list."
—*Elle*

"A study of music, imagination and the power of a mother's love."
—*Parade*

"Satisfying and sweet . . . Love, empathy and fear—as well as a yellow songbird—wind through this tale of an unbreakable bond between mother and child. The novel demonstrates Ms. Rosner's deep understanding of the terrors of the Holocaust."
—*Pittsburgh Post-Gazette*

"The book will help you escape the drudgery of solitude in your own home—and remember past beacons of hope during troubling times."   —ReadersDigest.com

"A riveting page-turner that will delight music lovers and please members of any book club."
                                          —*Hadassah Magazine*

"The power of a mother-daughter bond is beautifully portrayed against the backdrop of 1941 Poland."
                                          —WBUR's The ARTery

"Written in beautifully understated prose and tinged with magical elements, *The Yellow Bird Sings* is about the bonds between mothers and daughters, and the enduring power of music and storytelling even in the most devastating of times."   —*Chronogram*

"*The Yellow Bird Sings* pulled at all my heartstrings, then installed some more just to pull at those, too. Perhaps the most heartbreaking and moving WWII book since Markus Zusak's *The Book Thief* . . . Melancholic and musical, Rosner's narrative encapsulates the perseverance of hope even when it feels like hopelessness is all that's left."
                                          —Paperback Paris

"Rosner challenges the Holocaust with a touch of magic . . . clarifying a dangerous time and place even as she offers a vibrant, affecting portrait of the mother-daughter relationship."
                                          —*Library Journal* (starred review)

"In Shira and Róża, Rosner captures two souls in turmoil, chronicling their grief as well as their strength of will to overcome, their longing and even surprising triumphs . . . *The Yellow Bird Sings* keeps your heart in your throat, your eyes pricked with tears."   —*BookPage* (starred review)

"This stunning debut novel sings with the power of a mother's love and the heartbreaking risks she'll endure."

—*Booklist*

"A World War II story with a *Room*-like twist, one that also deftly examines the ways in which art and imagination can sustain us . . . This is a Holocaust novel, but it's also an effective work of suspense, and Rosner's understanding of how art plays a role in our lives, even at the worst of times, is impressive."   —*Kirkus*

"Moving . . . A wrenching chronicle."

—*Publishers Weekly*

"A beautiful book in so many ways. Like Shira's imaginary bird, Jennifer Rosner's prose is lilting and musical, yet her tale of war's grave personal reality is gripping, heartrending, and so very real."   —Lisa Wingate, author of *Before We Were Yours* and *Before and After*

"Music and love course through this beautiful novel, twin rivers of wonder. Jennifer Rosner has written a book that will break your heart, and then put it back together again, a little larger than before."

—Alex George, author of *A Good American*